I'm Not an Only Child

Secrets and Betrayal

D1519122

Abigail Herows

Table of Contents

I dedicate this book to my children. You know who you are.

I want you to know I have no secrets from you and would never do anything like this to you. You are too important to me, and I could never live without you in my life.

You never gave me nor your father an ounce of trouble, and we thank you for that. You made raising children easy for both of us, and we are so proud of the adults you have become. You are compassionate, accepting, bright, resourceful... I could go on and on.

You are much better people than I could ever be. I am amazed at your career choices and how easy you made them look when we all know that is the farthest thing from the truth. I wish you the long, healthy, happy, and successful life that you deserve.

You are the greatest accomplishment and gift in my life. I thank God for you every day. Love you forever.

* * *

Thank you also to my husband for supporting me on this project and for all the nights you had to sit alone because I was glued to my computer. Looking forward to a long retirement. ILY.

* * *

I also want to say a special thanks to Lynn for remembering all the events and details that I had forgotten. Thank you for the 60+ years of memories, and I'm looking forward to many more. Your friendship over the years has meant more to me than you will ever know (although you know more than most people). I can't thank you enough for being a part of my life. I love you dearly, sis.

* * *

To Sandy, my partner in crime. Thank you for sitting on that wall 55 years ago, waiting for me every night. We have been through so much together since then. Looking forward to more adventures with you. Love you, sis.

* * *

I would like to give one more recognition to my new friend, Faith. This project would not have been possible without you.

You know more about me in this short time than most people whom I've known for a lifetime. Thank you for your expertise, patience, and kindness. I'm amazed at how you always knew what I wanted to say before *I* knew what I wanted to say. Thank you for saying yes. I will always be grateful to you.

Prologue:

A New Chapter

Today is my father's birthday, which forces me to remember the death of my relationship with my mother.

As you'll soon discover, my dad will forever be one of the most patient, kind, and thoughtful people I know. I can't think of a better way to honor my love for him than by starting this book today. He, of all people, deserves it.

My relationship with my mom was quite different. Reflecting on the closeness of my relationship with my father makes me feel even more distant from my mother. Despite our shared blood, there were times when I could not feel more different from her. Actually, I don't think I've ever felt so different from *anyone*.

Today brings a bittersweet feeling.

Family is a funny thing. I don't mean that in the literal sense, although I'm sure some of you have hilarious relatives. What I mean by that is how unusual our relationships are with our family members. We're born into this world with an immediate, eternal connection with a select group of people simply because we share their genes. Plus, we tend to exhibit certain tendencies based on our upbringing with these individuals.

Parents add a particularly challenging layer to this enigma. The fact that they gave us life in the first place is a gift, and we're conditioned to think highly of them in our younger years. If we don't understand something as a kid, we'll often turn to our parents because we think, *Surely, they'll know what to do. They're grown-ups. They'll take care of it.* However, as we grow up and start to form our independent thoughts, we also see our parents as humans. Showing them mercy for their shortcomings is much easier for those blessed with good parents. But for those with a complicated relationship with their parents, it becomes clearer why that tension has existed for so long.

At the same time, though, we always feel slightly indebted to our parents, even as adults. We'll always be their children. However imperfectly they may have raised us, they're still responsible for helping us become the people we are today. We're forever subjected to their influence in our lives. Even for people whose parents left them at a young age, the absence of a parent has its kind of influence, too. Sometimes, we appreciate their influence. At other times, we resent them greatly for it.

I'm not exactly sure where I fall along that spectrum. Despite the ebbs and flows of my relationship with my parents—okay, with my mom—I can't help but feel connected to them... to *her*. I wish I didn't feel that way. If I could, I'd cut off all ties with her and never have to speak to her again. Moreover, I'd never feel *guilty* about never having to speak to her again. It would make my life so much easier if I never had to acknowledge my mom's role.

At least, that was my line of thinking for many years.

It has been a struggle to come to terms with my relationship with my mother. These feelings result from decades worth of painful memories and betrayals that have been weighing on my heart. But now, as I take time to ponder the subject, I can't help but wonder...

What does it mean to be a mother?

And what does it mean to be a family?

I reflected on these questions quite a bit when I started a family of my own. It was a significant role reversal that gave me flashbacks of my childhood and saw how my parents treated me and each other. I tried to detach myself from my upbringing and start fresh with my husband and children. My husband is a great provider, a good father, a big help around the house, not one to hang out in bars, and never one to stray, while my children are the most precious gifts I could've hoped for. And yet, I struggled to shake off the early memories of my mother's influence as I stepped into that role myself.

Overall, though, I was doing pretty well as I took on these new responsibilities. But a phone call I received at 54 changed my life forever.

Before that phone call, I'd had a lot of time to think about my thoughts about "family" in terms of my parents, given that I grew up as an only child. As a kid, I had no siblings in my house to bounce ideas off or run around with at a nearby park. I saw how the other kids in our neighborhood would play with and talk about their siblings, which made me yearn for one, too. I could still socialize with other kids just fine, but it wasn't the same as having a brother or a sister. It seemed like having a permanent best friend I could always be with. That would've been the best thing ever.

People I'd heard speak about family seemed truly happy with the families they had chosen. *Good for them,* I thought. *But how do they go about living a life with a chosen family when their immediate families are right there? Does "family" truly only consist of one's own flesh and blood?*

And what about my own family? How can I feel so close to some people yet so distant from others who are meant to play an equal role in my life? When I don't really feel like I'm a part of a family, where do I truly belong?

In order to answer that, I couldn't keep all of my thoughts to myself, which is why I've chosen to write this book. I still don't know if I'll be able to answer that last question by the end, but it's certainly worth trying to make sense of it. If nothing else, this will be a helpful opportunity to share my experience and try to make sense of everything. I just know that having all these ideas bounce around in my head for several years isn't doing anyone any favors.

I mentioned this above, but I want to reiterate that my husband and children have been nothing short of a miracle. Each one of them has been the kind of family I could've only prayed for, and even then, they've far exceeded any expectations I could've had. None of my confusion or frustration toward my struggles with the term "family" has to do with them. If anything, they are a source of redemption for the concept. They're a permanent reminder that it is possible to be loved in a family environment at the best and, especially, the worst of times. They always have my heart.

But as I continue to wrestle with the concept of family, I also want to stress that this journey is a work in progress, even if these words are printed in ink by the time you see them. I've reflected on this topic so much over the last couple of years, yet I feel there's still so much I don't know. Do you also find that sometimes? Life feels simpler when you don't know as much. I suppose that's why the mantra claiming that "ignorance is bliss" became so popular, even though it's dangerous to avoid seeking the truth. I certainly don't want to be ignorant, but I miss the days when morality appeared so black-and-white. Being kind to people was good; being mean to people was bad. When did that basic practice of human kindness get so complicated? *Especially* within one's own family?

There's so much I have yet to understand about relationships and family. My views of these topics might even change throughout this book due to reliving all those painful experiences. I already know it will take me a long time to write some of these chapters, and I'm not looking forward to doing it, but I will write them anyway. I've spent far too long harboring this heartache, and I have to get this off of my chest.

Although I'll be sharing my life, this book will focus on relational dynamics rather than the trajectory of my education or career. Those factors don't apply as frequently to my story, so I won't discuss them often here. I figured I'd made that pretty clear already, but I just wanted to ensure we were all on the same page.

Regardless of where this journey takes me (and therefore us), I want you to know that my thoughts are 100% my own. I promise you that this is not an attempt at forcing my beliefs down your throat, although I do hope there is some space for grace amid my story. I'm an imperfect person trapped in an imperfect situation—nay, a devastating situation. I'm merely doing my best to make sense of all of this information, and I appreciate your willingness to learn more about me.

At this point, I don't know if I'm ready to forgive my mother for what she has done. I just don't. I know that might not be the "proper" answer, but I'd be lying if I said anything different. I just want to be totally honest in letting you know my starting point. That said, this book isn't meant to be a vindictive revenge tale to get back at her for all the heartache she caused me. I want this to help me heal from these wounds and potentially help others heal. Who knows, perhaps that will change by the time I reach the end of this book. We'll have to see.

The vast majority of my life has been nothing short of wonderful. I've been blessed with many amazing friends and family members who have helped make this adventure a positive one. I don't want my story to sound like it has only been filled with "doom and gloom," but there will be times when this book will get quite dark. There have definitely been some more difficult things that have happened to me, and I don't want to shy away from the trauma they have caused. For so many years, I've tried to tell myself that I've had it pretty good, and while that has mostly been true, I don't want to hide the bad stuff away anymore.

I have never been so vulnerable with such a large audience. Well, okay, hold on… I don't mean to sound proud in assuming that this will be a widely-read book. My goal isn't to chase after fame and fortune; I have no interest in that, and if anything, the thought of gaining more attention through this is unnerving. I've never written a book before, and I don't plan on writing another one. This is it for me.

But I want to share my experiences with more people in hopes that it will offer a window into dysfunctional family dynamics. It's complicated, messy, and traumatic, and I wouldn't wish it on anyone. But I also believe we can expose this darkness by shining a light on it to provide the way out. It's only by following the light that we can truly see anything.

This began as a collection of journal entries only ever intended for my eyes to read. Writing my thoughts away was incredibly therapeutic and freed up space in my ever-busy mind. But as these stories began to form an overarching narrative, I started to get that nagging gut feeling that this wasn't meant to stay with me. *Other people could learn from this*, the little voice in my head said to me. Over time, it got progressively harder to ignore that voice.

So, here I am: A Northeastern wife and mom who wants to understand the meaning of family better. Call me crazy if you'd like, but I don't think I'm alone in wanting to learn more about that.

If my story could provide any kind of comfort or reassurance, I would consider that a huge blessing well beyond my capabilities. For those of you who have a relatively stable family life, I truly admire your curiosity in picking up my book, and thank you for opening up your mind to learning more about it. Every family has problems, and I want you to know that your presence is very much appreciated here.

And for those of you who have struggled with some form of severe family dysfunction, my heart especially goes out to you. I'm keeping you in my prayers as I weave this narrative together. I never want you to feel as lonely as I felt in that darkest period. You are not alone. Not now. Not ever.

I was 54 years old when my life fell apart. Here is my story to that point and beyond.

Happy birthday, Dad.

Enfield, Connecticut

Chapter 1:

Meeting the Neighbors

I've always been someone who kept herself busy.

I think that's largely due to my upbringing as my parents' only child. Naturally, I had to find ways of occupying myself and entertaining my wandering imagination. But during my younger years, I didn't have to look too far before a beautiful angel in the form of my best friend came into my life.

My earliest memories take place during our days in Enfield. It's a small town along the Connecticut-Massachusetts border where everybody knows and helps everybody. All in all, it was a typical small-town community (even if that meant knowing a little *too* much about everybody).

My parents got to know the townspeople pretty quickly, which meant that it didn't take long for them to meet me.

"Awe, now who's this little cutie here?" someone would ask my parents as they crouched down to meet my eye line.

"This is our pride and joy, Emma," my dad would tell them.

"Well, it's a pleasure to meet you, Miss Emma," they'd say.

I'd stick my chin out with as big a smile as I could let out without showing my teeth, usually met with a chuckle from the adults. It was nice to be welcomed in such a warm way. I had a feeling I'd be just fine in this town.

My parents bought a joint hardware convenience store there when I was three and we moved into the apartment right above it. Any homeowner needs to use tools at some point, and those were the days when people liked to take their time to discuss it over a face-to-face conversation.

We soon discovered that our building was located next to the home of an elderly couple named Joan and Walter. Both of them had gentle smiles and kind eyes that greeted us every time we stepped out the door. Joan's voice was as warm as a blanket while Walter's laughter could cure a cold. When they looked at me, it was like they were looking into my heart.

Joan and Walter made everyone feel like their presence mattered. They never made it seem like they were simply waiting for the conversation to be over to get back to what they were doing. Instead, the whole world stopped, and the only thing that mattered was whether or not I had fun at the playground that day. Naturally, this only made me want to spend more time with them.

If that wasn't already enough of a blessing, I soon discovered that Joan and Walter had a granddaughter who often came to visit them. And that was how I met Amy.

Amy and I got along famously from the start. We would play together every time she came up to visit her grandparents. Whether one of us had new toys to play with or we'd just let our imaginations run wild, there was never any shortage of games to play together. The time would pass so quickly when we were together that I wouldn't even realize when a full day had passed. I'm sure it was a nice relief for my parents to know that I was in safe hands with Joan and Walter, never mind all the fun I had with Amy.

Having been an only child, it was so nice to have another girl around to play with. It was always nice to have my parents' undivided attention, but it was different to get to play with somebody my age. At that age, just about any pairing of children would find something in common to bring them together, but it was deeper than that with Amy. We just "got" each other. We were totally on the same wavelength with everything. If she wanted to eat a snack, I wanted to eat a snack. If I wanted to look at the flowers, she wanted to look at the flowers. It was all that was needed to build a lasting friendship for a couple of three-year-olds.

That's definitely one of the elements of childhood that I missed greatly as I grew into adulthood. The strongest of friendships would often begin in the simplest of circumstances. Nothing ever felt forced with Amy. We didn't overanalyze the potential benefit we could reap from befriending the other person; we didn't even know to look for that sort of thing. We just lived close by and wanted to build and live in our imaginary worlds together. And that was enough.

I think a lot of adults could stand to learn from that sort of simplicity at times. Seeking common ground and choosing to see the good in people can eliminate a lot of unnecessary conflicts. But while children might see things in a more simplistic, black-and-white scenario, it heightens those emotions. That means the good tends to feel especially good, and the bad tends to feel especially bad.

Case in point, I had thick, curly hair that would've been tough to brush for a seasoned pro. I wasn't experienced in hair-brushing techniques, so I would see if my mom was willing to help me do it.

"Mommy, can you brush my hair?" I'd ask.

Deep sigh. Eye roll. "Sit down," she barked.

Eager to avoid disappointment, I followed her orders. I plunked myself down on the nearest stepstool as my mother got out the skinny, plastic hairbrush. She pushed her left hand on the top of my head while using her right hand to dig the brush into my head. She yanked the bristles down in spastic bursts, inching her way through the length of my hair.

"Ow!" I yelled. "Mommy, that hurts!"

"Shut up," my mom retorted, ripping through a new strand of hair. "Your whining isn't gonna make your hair any softer."

We went through this cycle a couple of times. The repeated digs into my scalp and pulling on my hair gave me a headache as I watched my tears spill onto the floor. When she got tired of hearing me scream, she'd finish whatever bundle of knots she was working on and hand me the brush.

"If you're gonna complain about it so much, then just go to Joan's and make her do it," she hissed. And she'd walk out of the bathroom. I'd try to hold in my tears until I knew she was gone.

Even in those early days, I could sense that my mom had a very different demeanor than my dad. Everybody who knew Dad was drawn to him. If he had been the subject of a TV show, *Everybody Loves Raymond* would've needed a different name by the time the '90s rolled around because everybody loved Dad first. He taught me how to tell time and ride a bike, and he'd build houses for me out of Play-Doh. Having been around tools for his work, he was quite adept at forming little people and furniture out of Play-Doh to fill up the houses. I was always amazed at how realistic they were. I treasured those memories dearly.

Dad was the kind of guy to eat every cake I'd bake for him in my Easy Bake Oven (although, looking back, I'm not too sure how thoroughly the lightbulb had cooked those desserts). He'd use a tiny plastic fork to cut his ant-sized portion, stick it in his mouth, and pretend to fall off his chair because "it was too delicious." It made me belly laugh every time.

My mom's reaction?

"I would never eat that shit."

For a young girl, those were some of the most haunting words that could be spoken to her. It wasn't even necessarily the use of profanity because I was far too young to understand the magnitude of that specific word. But the knowledge that my mother would never want to eat anything I'd made for her crushed me. Because of these kinds of moments, I started to think that my mother didn't like me. Understandably so.

So, when my mom got tired of brushing my hair, she'd ship me off to Joan and Walter's house. My parents liked them, and they also became friends with Amy's parents, Rose and Jim, when Amy and I became friends. It worked out well that the parents and grandparents got along so well because I ended up spending a lot of time with Joan and Walter, even when Amy wasn't around.

When I'd show up at their place, Joan would see me standing there with red eyes and a half-brushed head of hair.

"Oh, come in, sweetie," she'd welcome me inside. "Let's finish brushing that lovely hair of yours."

Joan ushered me into her bathroom to finish the job that my mother had half-heartedly started. Much like her smile, Joan was so gentle with the brush. Somehow, she found a way to slide the bristles through my knotty mane without having me writhe in pain. It was a much smoother process with her than with my mother. Her words were so tender and loving, always trying to soothe any hint of discomfort I'd experience along the way. I imagined this was what it was like in the movies when a maternal figure brushed a little girl's hair.

Looking back, I think Joan appreciated having a girl around all the time to dote on in these small ways. Joan only had one child, Rose, who was well past the stage of living at home. And while Amy came to visit often, it wasn't the same as having a little one around all the time. I think it made Joan happy to be able to play both the "mom" and "grandma" roles more often.

It was around this time that I started calling her Grandma Joan. It only made sense to call her husband, Grandpa Walter, who was also well deserving of that title.

But it wasn't as though I had no biological grandparents, either—my dad's mom was the kindest, sweetest, and most generous person in the whole world. She was a religious woman with the biggest heart. She didn't have much, but she always shared what she did have, which made her much richer than those who were financially well off. Not to mention, she was the best cook ever! Even now, I try to emulate her cooking methods at home, although there's nothing quite like grandma's cooking. I hope to be half the person she was because she was just that remarkable.

Of course, that didn't sit well with my mom. Whenever we'd drive home after going to my grandma's place for dinner, my mother would have something negative to say about the food. "That sauce was soupy. Why would she bother serving that?" "Her soup was salty. I've never liked her soup." "Those meatballs were so bland; it's like she's never heard of salt."

There was never anything wrong with the food. It was pure jealousy. My mother simply did not like someone else getting all the praise and attention. Even still, I loved that we got to see my grandmother often, although it was nice to have grandparent-type figures as our neighbors, too.

Before too long, I would get just as excited to see Grandma Joan and Grandpa Walter as Amy (well, maybe not quite that much, but it was pretty close). It was nice to have grandparent-type figures who were so close by and loved me as their own grandchild.

Like my dad's mom, Grandma Joan was wonderful at cooking tasty dishes for me and Amy. One of my personal favorites was omelets; she'd spread grape jelly over them and roll them into little cylinders. It may not sound tempting, but we always thought it was the best breakfast ever. Everything she cooked had this comforting touch to it that made me feel like I was at home. But this particular meal had a special place in my heart, and I knew I had to remember it.

Grandpa Walter, on the other hand, would always be willing to play with us when Amy and I would play imaginative games. Her grandparents had a lovely and spacious front porch where we'd often play school. Grandpa Walter would help set us up with actual school desks to mimic the feeling of being in school. We felt like the big kids since we were too young to be in school at that point. He would call himself Miss Marilyn and pretend to be our teacher. Thankfully, he was a very kind teacher who didn't give lots of homework. I think my later teachers could've learned a lesson or two from Miss Marilyn.

But school wasn't the only game Amy and I would play together. Sometimes, on the front steps, we'd play "Bank" using the leaves from the bushes. We'd pluck them off the plants and pretend they'd be pieces of change that we'd swap out with one another. Naturally, the big leaves would be the dollar bills, and the small leaves would be quarters, nickels, and pennies. It makes me nostalgic just thinking of it. Kids are so creative. They can make a game or scenario using just about anything. I mean, leaves as coins? If only my actual bank used the same form of currency.

As we grew to the ripe old age of four, Amy and I started taking on some big girl responsibilities. Grandma Joan and Grandpa Walter would rent out the top floor of their house to various tenants, and on occasion, Amy and I would go upstairs and dust for them. They thought it was fun to give us a job, and we loved being up there. Being four years old and all, I'm sure you could imagine the job we did. I think we made the air even dustier than it had been before we went up there.

But at the end of the day, we put in some solid hours of hard work; the tenants would compensate us appropriately. Our pay for dusting was each earned a small, flower-shaped piece of soap. Each piece was so unique to us. The only soap we had ever known of was ivory soap. We adored the smell and shape of the flower soap, and it only made us want to keep going back and doing it all over again the next day. It was so much better than money (other than leaf money, of course).

And there were few things as exciting as sitting on the sidewalk with Amy every Monday, waiting for the Wonder Bread man to make his delivery. It was like waiting for the ice cream truck; only we didn't have to rush to eat our food out of fear that it would melt down the sides of our hands. When the bread man showed up, he would always have a miniature loaf of Wonder Bread ready to give us. It was the greatest joy to be thought of in such a sweet and delicious way. We quite literally thought that was the best thing since sliced bread.

I had such lovely times getting to know Amy and her family while living in Enfield. They went beyond the role of typical neighbors and turned out to be the healthy and loving family that I never had. I mean, I had half of a loving family, but the strains with my mother were already starting to form. I felt an ease with Amy's family that I didn't feel with my own.

Those early childhood memories are so vivid for me, for better and worse. I'm thankful I had the good times to balance out the more negative ones. No one has a perfect life, but I'm grateful for my upbringing. All in all, it was a pretty wonderful way to grow up.

Unfortunately, the robbery of my parents' store prevented me from continuing to live that idyllic early life.

Chapter 2:

Where There's Smoke...

We weren't prepared to be robbed.

To be fair, robberies don't seem like what most people could be prepared for. Sure, some people might have more protective measures in place to prevent a potential thief from successfully stealing anything. I suppose they're "prepared," but that really only covers the logistical possibility of a robbery. But it's a totally different thing to be around when a hooded figure shows up at their door, demands that they give up all their money, and have the lives of their loved ones threatened. They could take all the precautions in the world, but I don't think many of them would be physically prepared to act in that instance. If anything, they might be even more jittery if they're depending on external means to protect them because if those devices fail, it's bad news.

I think someone must come from an incredibly tense background if they're mentally prepared to be robbed. The moment of a break-in is terrifying. It stuns you. It confuses you. It goes against the natural order of the place you're in... At least, that was the case with Enfield. It wasn't a place where people go with the expectation of having to watch their backs. If that were the case, there was no way I could wander over to Grandma Joan and Grandpa Walter's place all the time. People move to Enfield to get out of the big cities and enjoy the slower pace of life, casually greeting passers-by as they roam the streets. It's a place where people intentionally go to get away from metropolitan struggles like, well, crime. But I suppose no town is immune to it.

Amy and I were meandering around my parents' store one day, just as we would on any other weekday. We still weren't of age to be in full-time school, so it wasn't uncommon for one or both sets of parents to watch over us during the day. Business was carrying on as usual, and there wasn't anything particularly spectacular about the day, which truly made it the time we least expected a robbery.

BOOM!

The loud noise caused everyone's heads to whip toward the front door. Two men wearing dark clothing had blasted it open so the door had banged against the wall. The men wasted little time finding the cash register. Each step they took felt like it was shaking the entire building floor as they pounded their way to the check-out counter.

Then, they each pulled out a gun.

This was now an armed robbery. And one of the men pointed his weapon directly at my mother's head.

"Here's what's gonna happen," one of the men said to her. "You're gonna shut up and give me all the cash in that register, and nobody'll get hurt. I'm gonna know if you miss one bill, so you'd better not think of tricking me."

Even though I was still very young when this happened, it was the first time in my life that I'd ever seen my mother looking truly scared.

Before I had time to process what was happening (as best as possible), I felt a cold, dry hand wrap around my upper arm. I looked up to see that the other robber had grabbed Amy and me and started marching us to the back of the store.

"Dad! Mom! Dad! Help!" I tried to yell my way free, but it was no use. There was no way the two of us were breaking free. My heart was pounding so hard, and I had no idea why the mean man was taking us away. The only thing my mom and dad could do was sneak a glance at us through the corners of their eyes before the first robber started talking again.

"You wouldn't want anything to happen to those precious girls, would you?" He taunted them. "So, you'd better give me my damn money before anybody gets hurt."

My parents could only listen to Amy and me scream as the second robber stole us away.

The robber pulled us along at a faster pace than our legs could move until they found a small supply closet in one of the back corners of the store. He yanked the doors open to release a wall of strong, soapy odors. The closet was full of detergents and soaps that almost burned the nose if someone stood too close to them.

Despite Amy and me fighting back as best as we could, the robber placed his hands on our backs and shoved us into the closet.

"Stay here, and don't move," he ordered.

With that, he closed the door and locked us inside.

Amy and I dared not say a word to each other. It was dark, and our tiny bodies were crammed into an even smaller space than we were suited for. We tried to find a comfortable position amidst all the bottles and boxes, but we kept on sliding around. It was hard enough to move around, but we were also terrified of making too much noise and risking getting into more trouble.

Neither one of us understood what was happening or why those bad men were locking us away and threatening to hurt my parents. Looking back, I don't think my parents understood what was happening, either, but we didn't know that at the time. All Amy and I knew was that we had been given clear instructions by men who looked like they could hurt us real bad if they wanted to. We just gripped onto each other's hands and whimpered out a few tears, trying desperately to stay quiet so as to not cause trouble.

I had no idea what was about to happen to my parents or our store, but I was so glad Amy was there with me. If I had been by myself, I'm sure I would've feared the situation that much more. But having her with me ensured that I wasn't alone in the midst of the ordeal. We certainly didn't feel safe, but it was a little bit safer knowing the other person was there, too.

I heard the robber's footsteps echo through the floor, and it was clear that he was walking back toward the rest of the adults. From there, any hints of the events taking place were filtered through a wooden closet door and a mental state of panic. The robbers kept telling people to "Shut up!" even when nobody was saying anything. Dad had tried to reason with them, and I believe he said something along the lines of "We don't want to cause anybody any trouble here." He always tried to be the peacemaker, even with the people who deserved it the least. Despite his best efforts, the robbers were not in any cooperative mood.

After a few muffled voices exchanged back and forth for a while, one of the robbers finally yelled "GO!" as his gun cocked. A few footsteps proceeded toward me and Amy, and my heart practically leaped into my throat. Were they coming over here? I wasn't ready for this to happen.

The footsteps quickly took on a more pointed, stomping sound moving progressively higher above our heads. They were forcing my parents up the stairs.

A few seconds passed with more footsteps shuffling around up there, some yelling to "hurry up." Even though I was still petrified, every subsequent threat these guys made had less and less of an effect on me. Looking back, I hate how I was being normalized to this situation so quickly. I'm just glad I didn't have to witness them threatening my parents upstairs, although that may have eased my active imagination.

Soon, two sets of footsteps ran down the stairs and out the door. Car doors opened and closed as the tires screeched into the distance. I guess they weren't actually concerned with the closet in the back after all.

Then, silence.

Amy and I had probably been in the closet for about 20 minutes at this point, but from our perspective, it felt like an eternity. Our bodies were starting to cramp up, and we desperately wanted to get out of there, but neither of us was willing to call out for help. We were going to follow the robber's orders until told otherwise.

Eventually, we heard my parents plunk their way down the stairs and move closer to the closet. After fidgeting the key into the lock, Dad opened the door to let Amy and me out.

"Are you guys okay?" He tried to console us, but I think he was trying to comfort himself just as much. He hugged us close to his chest, gripping our backs. "I'm so sorry. You should've never been caught in the middle of that. I love you so much. You're safe now."

It turned out that the robbers had been holding my parents at gunpoint the entire time. My dad thought they never truly wanted to hurt anybody but just wanted our money. The store's safe was located upstairs, so the robbers forced them to go there. Once they got what they wanted, the thieves were out of there in a flash. Thankfully, no one was physically hurt.

As I hugged my dad, I looked up and saw my mother. She wasn't making eye contact with me but just crossing her arms and staring off into the distance. There wasn't really much for her to see over there—just a few hammers and other tools. She might've been thinking about how they could've used those to harm us, but I doubt it. I think she was rattled that someone had put her in such a vulnerable spot, and there was nothing she could've done about it.

While I certainly don't want to belittle her trauma or response, I remember being slightly puzzled by it. She made no effort to see if anyone else was okay. She may have needed time to process everything herself, which would be totally fair. But she never checked in on Amy or me afterward, and I don't remember her doing that with my dad, either (at least, not while I was around). It was in little ways like that which caused me to question my mother's love for me or even my dad.

If I tried to be as objective as possible, I could see why he might've been interested in her when they were younger. I'd heard stories about how she had an exuberant personality. She was always the life of the party. Everyone loved to be around her, much like they did with Dad. He was a lot more mild-mannered than she was, but they both had this magnetism that drew others toward them. When they got together, it made a lot of sense to those who knew both of them. They thought my parents were such a cute couple that made a lot of sense, and they fully supported their relationship. What they didn't know was that it was a front that my mother put up when she was in public.

My mother was a completely different person when she was at home. It resulted in a lot of gaslighting or pretending that her imagined reality was the actual truth when it wasn't. She always wanted to be the center of attention and have everyone like her. But it wasn't just that she had to be liked—she had to be liked *the most*. Therefore, anyone whom she perceived to be more popular was an immediate threat in her mind. I noticed that she always had friends throughout her life but never really kept them for a long time. They would come and go very swiftly, and when they were gone, we'd never hear about them again.

But to make matters worse, she'd do everything in her power never to let anyone see that demanding, controlling, and manipulative side of her. I always felt so bad for Dad when the two of them went to parties together. Every time, she would drink way too much to the point where he'd practically have to carry her back to the car. He didn't want to, but he didn't think he had any other choice because he was a decent man. He never got to enjoy himself because he always had to babysit her. I never understood why she felt the need to drink so much when they went out, but she clearly didn't consider how much of a burden it put on my dad. He was far more patient with her than I would've been.

So, when the robbery ordeal was over, Dad probably appreciated having a few moments to focus solely on Amy and me without my mother breathing down his neck about something. It wasn't beyond her to complain about how he had done something wrong to allow something like this to happen, but we all appreciated the silence for a while.

Neither Amy nor I could get the smell of detergent from us for a long time. It was in our clothes, hair, and nostrils constantly. Some of it may have been a perceived smell after a while, but wow, did it linger.

Unfortunately, that wasn't the worst smell that lingered from the store.

One year later, my family went away for a little weekend trip. When we came back, we discovered that a fire had broken out and the store had completely burned down. Horrendous smells of smoke, ash, and various torched objects absolutely reeked as we just stared at the fallen remnants of our former way of life.

It was devastating. Our family lost almost everything we had worked so hard to achieve through that store. My parents had left behind so much to allow us to try to build something special in Enfield, and in the span of a few hours, everything had been burned to a crisp. As for me, I lost my first bicycle. It was a beautiful shade of pink with training wheels and lovely streamers dangling off the handlebars. I'd only just gotten it the previous week and was so excited to ride it, but it stood no chance against the fire. Nothing was salvageable.

I never knew the cause of the fire, but I've heard rumors over the years that suggested some pretty sketchy behavior. It could've been a premeditated attack on the store. I hate to even say this, but I've heard through the grapevine and some family members that my parents intentionally went away for the weekend because this had all been planned out. It may have been a deliberate attempt at arson. I was never told that for sure, though, so I've always been left to speculate on what actually happened. It has been a mystery to me ever since.

I have no idea how some people can feel the need to do such wicked and cruel things. What would compel someone to see a quaint, local business and feel the need to demolish it in such a horrible fashion? I don't know if they realize that it's not just a building that they're burning down, but that it's someone's livelihood and a valuable resource for community members. It's much more than some wooden planks and pillars. It's a reminder of home.

By the time my parents reviewed the damages, they had realized that it would be far too steep a cost to rebuild everything all over again. They were still a young couple with a young child to consider, and they didn't exactly have the most disposable income to throw at a huge project like this. If they were going to spend such a large sum of money, they figured it would be best to move to a new place altogether.

I don't remember much of the move itself, but I was heartbroken to leave all my wonderful memories behind. I didn't know when I'd see Grandma Joan or Grandpa Walter again. Or Amy. My beautiful best friend Amy. My chest hurt to think about having to be separated from her potentially. When would I see her? We'd have to stay in contact somehow. We just had to. But I couldn't believe this was happening.

Thankfully, my parents ended up moving to a new city that was only about a 30-minute drive away from Enfield. We had been knocked down, but we certainly weren't out.

Hartford, Connecticut

Chapter 3:

Lobster Claws

We moved to Hartford after the fire.

It was nice to be relatively close to the life we had in Enfield, but at the same time, it felt like that life was still out of reach. So close, yet so far. I suppose it was enough incentive for my parents to want to start completely fresh in a new city, as hard as I'm sure it was to pick all the remaining pieces up and start over again. Dad took up a job driving a dump truck, and while he still got to work with his hands, it was very different from the work he'd done before. I heard a fair bit about the challenges of that transition later in life, but I'm sure my parents still kept a lot of that pain from me. I couldn't imagine how difficult that period of life must've been for them.

But from my perspective at the time, I didn't realize everything that was happening. I was sad to leave Amy, Grandma Joan, and Grandpa Walter, but I also knew I had no choice. So, I just followed my mother and father to Hartford and prepared myself for what that town had in store as best I could.

Hartford was a bigger city compared to Enfield, and we certainly didn't know all the townspeople by name. That said, it still wasn't exactly a large place, so the adjustment felt a bit more manageable. All in all, it wasn't too dramatic of a transition for us, especially since we had lived in Connecticut for a while. We had enough to keep us going and make do each day, and that's more than a lot of other people can say.

By the time we moved, I was finally old enough to start going to full-time school. My first experience of that world was kindergarten, which I attended at the nearby public school. I don't have a ton of memories from kindergarten, although I do remember crying on my first day. All the other kids were crying, too, but the difference was that while they cried because they *wanted* to go home, I cried because I *had* to go home. What does that say about my home life? But in spite of that reaction, kindergarten itself wasn't too eventful. Sometimes, no news is good news, and this was definitely one of those times. The fact that it was an unremarkable time in my life just meant that I suppose I'd adapted relatively well to that change of environment. I'll take that.

Grade school, on the other hand, was a much different story.

I transferred to a Catholic school in the next town over at the start of first grade. On the first day of school, my mother went with me to school to get situated with everything. My mother would speak to various nuns who ran the school and taught all the subjects. Meanwhile, as a six-year-old, I was more curious about why the nuns were wearing those black and white robes than the structure of the school day.

But at one point in the conversation, one of my mother's comments caused me to snap right out of my imagination. The nun/teacher talked about something to do with discipline or following orders with my mom, who told her, in no uncertain terms, "Don't think twice about hitting Emma if she needs it."

What parent says that? At least, what *good* parent says that?

It's one thing to hit or spank your own children as a corrective action (though I have my own thoughts on that), but it's something totally different to allow another adult to do it. This teacher was a woman I'd never met in my life before and therefore didn't trust, and my mother instantly gave her permission to physically hurt me. But it wasn't just that my mom passively permitted it to happen after the fact, either; she actually encouraged the nun to hit me whenever she felt like it was appropriate. It sickens me to think about how twisted that was.

The thought of being treated by the nuns this way was horrifying. I wasn't the type of child to act up. The reason why I could last for as long as I did in the closet in the Enfield robbery is that I was a softer personality who was terrified of breaking the rules, even when I didn't know what the rules were. For instance, when I was seven, my mom asked her cousin to drive me somewhere, even though she knew he'd been drinking the whole day. He was stone-cold drunk. He drove so erratically, and even though I didn't know the rules of the road, I knew this was a scary ride. But I was terrified to say anything because of the punishment I'd get from my mother over talking back to her cousin. So, you put that quiet, shy first grader in a new school, surrounded by strict nuns for the first time in her life, and she would be seriously scared. And I was just that.

I think that was the first and last time my mother showed her face at school until I graduated from eighth grade. She wouldn't have wanted any more involvement in my life than was absolutely necessary. If boarding school had been an option for us, it wouldn't have surprised me if she had considered that so that she could ship me off for years. But I had to come home eventually, finding my way by myself.

The Catholic school was much further from my house than the public school had been. I walked to and from school every day, about a three-mile trip each way. It didn't matter if it was raining, snowing, or whatever the conditions were; I walked the entire way every time. It certainly taught me about hard work and fending for myself at a young age. Of course, I had to be good at doing that anyway as an only child, but it just solidified that I had to be independent and start looking after myself very early on.

But hey, that's not to say that my mother didn't help out at all: She did give me a Carnation Breakfast Essentials drink for breakfast every day. For those who don't know, it's basically a chocolate-flavored protein drink, although I believe it's available in children's cereal flavors like Frosted Flakes and Fruit Loops now.

"Emma, you're not gonna find a better breakfast out there," she'd boast. I knew she only thought that way because it was fast and easy, but she never admitted that to me. "Hurry up and drink it."

So, I'd gulp down my glorified chocolate milk and walk three miles to school with all that liquid sloshing around in my stomach. Between that and lunch, it was enough to get me through the day. Plus, by the time I got to school and saw all of my friends, I didn't think as much about what was sitting in my stomach. I loved spending time with my friends during recess and lunch breaks. We'd swap stories from the classroom and play different games together. I just wished that I had that same kind of friend network once the bell rang at the end of the day.

I couldn't see most of my school friends after school since they lived in the same town as the school while I lived a bit further. That really bummed me out because I got along pretty well with them. My mother wasn't exactly the type of person to set up playdates, either, so school was really the best chance I had to see them. I missed out on a lot of extra social time there.

Do you ever have those *what if* moments where you just speculate on how some things would've turned out if something had happened differently? My relationship with my Catholic school friends was one of those moments for me. I knew it wasn't the end of the world that I didn't see them as often, but it was a bit disappointing to think about the friendships that could've amounted from that school. I wasn't necessarily worried about being popular or anything, but I loved having close friends. I always enjoyed socializing with my peers because I didn't have as many opportunities to do that at home. People with siblings had not only the siblings themselves but also the friends of their siblings to interact with, which I didn't have. I could've very easily seen myself being closer to some of my former peers if I'd spent more time with them, but that never really happened.

Fortunately, I had a lot of other friends in my own neighborhood. Don't get me wrong, I didn't mind being by myself (when it was my choice), and I always looked forward to spending time with Amy. There was just something extra special about having a whole group of friends. Nothing can replace the feeling of hanging out with a bunch of people your age and talking about the stuff that kids care about—playgrounds, toys, and the like. We had so much fun sprinting out of our front doors and meeting in the street before deciding what we were going to do or explore next.

Unfortunately, I also didn't get to see them as much as I would've liked to. They went to the local public school and didn't get much homework, whereas I had a ton of homework to do every night. It took a long time to do and was hard to grasp, but every night after coming home from work, Dad would help me do it. I have such distinct memories of him sitting at the kitchen table with me and sharpening my pencil with a kitchen knife, which I thought was pretty cool. He then proceeded to talk me through my math homework, and it always made way more sense after he explained it. I'm so thankful for his patience with me. I would've loved to have him as a piano teacher.

I took piano lessons at the convent with a nun every day after school. By this point, I was scared to death of the nuns. When my mom made that comment about allowing them to hit me, I didn't realize that this was well within the typical means of discipline for them. Back in those days, the nuns were allowed to hit you. And they did. Hard.

Every afternoon, I dreaded the final bell. Not only was I being isolated from my friends until the next morning, but I had to deal with the piano teacher. In a school full of nuns who were sticklers for the rules—and remember, this is coming from a rule follower—this nun was especially mean. I questioned whether or not she had something against me personally or whether she was like this with everyone. When it's a one-on-one environment, it's harder to tell.

After the bell went off, I scurried as fast as I could to the convent. I dared not be late for my lesson. But I always happened to catch the eye of another nun or two who'd scold me for moving in an "unladylike manner" or something like that.

"Emma! Stop running around like a deranged child."

I can still hear their comments in my head because of how absolutely nonsensical they sounded. Wasn't I a child? Why couldn't I run like one? Plus, if I had to choose between being late for my piano lesson or running like a deranged child, you'd bet I'd run like a deranged child.

I'd arrive at the piano and hurriedly start my warm-up sequence. A few minutes later, I'd hear footsteps coming toward the piano as the nun entered the room.

"Page 34!" She hadn't even sat on the bench yet and was already yelling orders at me. I scrambled to find the page as quickly as I could, but I'd get so nervous that I found it hard to flip the pages. They always seemed to stick to each other at the wrong moments.

"Can't you read, child?" She'd scold me. "Thirty-four, the one after thirty-three. Hurry up!"

Once I'd finally get to the correct page, she'd make her way to the bench with a ruler in her right hand. She'd initiate me to start the piece, and with my heart racing at a hundred miles an hour, I'd do my best to play it. I'd try so hard. Everything would go smoothly at first, but after a few bars…

WHACK!

She slammed the ruler onto my knuckles.

"E-flat, not E. From the top."

I'd start again, paying close attention to the upcoming E-flat, trying to concentrate—

WHACK!

"Have you gone mad? You just played the correct note a second ago. It's clearly an A! Are you trying to waste my time?"

"No, Sister, I'm not," I'd yelp out, trying to hold back tears.

"Well, then, play it properly this time. From the top, once more."

I'd start again and inevitably mess up somewhere along the way.

WHACK!

"Stupid child. Again!"

WHACK!

"Again!"

WHACK!

My knuckles would be swollen and bruised by the end of the lesson. I wanted to massage them so badly, but it would only put more pressure on those bluish-purple lumps. The lessons were always so nerve-racking, and I couldn't enjoy the process of learning piano at all.

But with chores waiting for me when I got home, it wasn't exactly like I had much to look forward to there, either.

After finishing my piano lesson, I'd come back home to have dinner. Right around the time that dinner had ended, my neighborhood friends would always wait outside my house for me to come out and play with them. My mother would go up to the door, tell them, "She's too busy to play tonight," and close it. They would just slowly backstep away from our front door and carry on playing. I was always so confused as to why they all had so much more playtime than I did, but my mom never let me go out with them.

Instead of playing outside, I had to do the dinner dishes. Night after night, it became a routine for my friends to wait for me outside to play with them after dinner. They weren't expecting anything unreasonable; we were still far too young to even think about getting up to any shenanigans. They just wanted to run around and play imaginary games until it got dark, and they had to go back inside. But night after night, I had to wash the dishes, and my mom would send the kids away. To put it in perspective, I was at an age where I wasn't even tall enough to reach the sink while standing on my tippy toes. I'd have to stand on a stool.

My mother would start the process by rinsing the dishes and soaking them in scalding hot water.

"Wash these, will ya?" She'd demand of me, motioning toward the dishes at the bottom of the sink.

I'd stare at the dishes down there and observe these thin, almost sparkly waves rising from the sink. I knew that that meant there was some kind of steam coming up from the water, meaning that it would be very, very hot.

"It's too hot," I'd explain.

"No, it's not," She'd fire back.

"But I'll get hurt."

"No, you won't. Just do it."

"But what if I burn myself?"

"Just shut up and do it! Stop being a wuss. The water's fine. You never do anything to help around here!"

So, just like it was with the piano teacher, I'd fight back the tears as I plunged my hands into the water. It was far too hot to touch. The water must've been just short of boiling at that point. I'd move my hands as quickly as I could in and out of the sink to spare them from burning right off.

By the time I'd finished up, my hands were bright red and throbbing with pain. Between the swollen knuckles and the red skin, they practically looked like lobster claws. It was dreadful to think about having to go back to my room and hold a pencil for hours as I tried to finish all my homework after that.

And then, I'd repeat everything again the next day, rain or shine, snow or sleet. It would get pretty cold during the winters in Connecticut, and I remember one season in particular when I had really chapped lips. I'd wanted to relieve that discomfort, so I thought I'd ask my mother for help.

"Mom, my lips are chapped. Can you buy me Chapstick?" I asked her.

"No," she responded. "Let this be a lesson to you to stop licking your lips."

It didn't matter how infrequently I licked my lips—the weather was too stinking cold, and my lips just dried out. I knew that I would have to be pretty independent as an only child, but this reminded me that I wasn't going to be getting a lot of support from my mother.

I have lots of fond memories of my childhood, but they're slightly tainted by a select few adults who seemed dead set on making my life miserable. I'd almost grown accustomed to authority figures who'd been unjustifiably harsh on me without ever getting to really know me. It caused me to fear the worst-case scenario before I even got to know a new teacher or adult of some kind. This wasn't universally the case, though—thank goodness for people like Dad and my grandmother, who showed me what it meant to have the loving warmth a kid is supposed to experience. They were definitely a key reason why I had any belief that someone in a position of authority could be kind to me.

I'm also incredibly grateful for the friendships I've formed over the years, even if they could've been something more enduring. For the season of life that they were around, they were fantastic. But after a few years of settling into my routine, I did get another friend to spend time with—a furry, excitable friend who barked at the door whenever I came home.

Chapter 4:

Tucker

I was eight years old when I got my puppy, Tucker.

He was the most beautiful Sheltie I'd ever seen in my young life. His long, pointed snout made every glance he took appear intentional and focused. Yet, his elongated facial features were paired with short- to medium-sized legs poking from the bottom of his fluffy midsection. In this sense, he felt like the best kind of hybrid between a majestic prince and an adorable youngling.

And his fur. Oh, my goodness. The brown and white strands were so thin on their own, but his fur was so thick and dense from all these strands being packed so closely together. When Tucker brushed past you or sat on you, you didn't want him to leave. It was so warm and smooth that it was unbelievably satisfying to the touch. He felt like one of those big blankets someone might find at their grandparents' cottage and drape over themselves while sitting in front of a fire. Just the softest thing I'd ever laid my hands on.

I remember the day we picked him up from the shelter. I was so giddy with excitement at the thought of getting a puppy, but seeing him in person made the experience real. My parents let him sit in the back seat with me for the drive back home, where I could let him out of his crate. We positioned him so that he'd rest on my lap, where he curled into an itty, bitty, beautiful fluffball. I immediately embraced this living blanket of a dog by gently stroking his amazing fur. He'd occasionally poke his head up so that he'd be looking right at me. His eyes were the most magnificent shade of blue, almost bordering on steel gray, and they'd gaze into my own. And just like that, we had an inseparable bond.

When he looked at me, it felt like I was his whole world. Suddenly, no one else was around except for the two of us as I kept petting his back. There was something about the expression on Tucker's face that struck the perfect balance between being playful and consoling. It was almost like he'd simultaneously want to chase after a ball while comforting me as I cried.

And I definitely cried. In fact, I couldn't stop crying when we first got him. I was so overwhelmed with happiness that my face couldn't physically prevent all of that emotion from leaking out. I was also in a state of disbelief to think that my parents actually let me have a dog at home. It wasn't like I had to do much convincing them or anything, but it just seemed surreal to me to think that I finally had my own buddy at home. Tucker felt like the closest thing I'd have to a sibling, and it was so exciting to have a companion around. I can't really explain it, but I just knew that I had made another amazing friend.

That's not to say it was smooth sailing the whole time we had him, though. He wasn't the easiest puppy to raise. Then again, *is* there such a thing as an "easy" puppy, especially in the first few weeks of having one? In some ways, it's almost harder than having a newborn baby because puppies can move around more easily when you're not looking. It takes a human baby much longer to learn how to get themselves from Point A to Point B, and while that requires its own kind of patience, it's hard to train a dog that just wants to move.

Puppies are almost always getting into something they shouldn't be getting into, and Tucker was no exception. If he hadn't been outside in a while, he'd run laps inside and bark at just about anything with legs. He'd also stick his snout into our shoes, jump on the couch, and eat his own dog bowls—not the food, but the bowls themselves. Naturally, that meant that food would end up in various places outside of the bowl that wasn't his mouth. But I still loved him, even if he was a little mischievous. It was all part of the deal of getting a puppy, and if keeping him meant that I had to look after him a bit more closely, then I was certainly prepared to do that.

My parents and I eventually found our routine in terms of caring for Tucker. Because I would be away at school during the day, my responsibility with him came at night. Once I finished up the dinner dishes, I'd take Tucker for a walk around the block. Dad would come along, which made the chore of dog walking much more enjoyable.

As we were walking along the street behind ours, we often came across a girl my age who looked really excited to see a dog. This girl would be standing along the front wall of her house, rocking forward and backward as she waited for us to come by with Tucker. When she'd spot us, she'd scurry her way over until she was about a foot away from our dog.

"Awe, he's so cute! Can I pet him?" She looked up at my dad with hopeful eyes.

Dad dipped his head down and up again. "Of course! His fur is pretty soft, isn't it?"

"Yeah!" She remarked as she stroked his fur for a few moments.

That was how I met my friend, Carin.

The two of us began seeing each other more regularly and playing together. Carin would come out of her house with her case of Matchbox cars while I'd come out with my Barbie dolls. Even though we liked different things, we just enjoyed being together and playing with our different toys. We quickly became the best of friends.

And my dad would get in on the action, too. Whenever he needed to take our car in for an inspection, he always wanted to be the first in line, so he'd leave the house at the crack of dawn. Carin and I would often go with him. We thought it was so exciting leaving our house in the dark. Plus, Dad would stop off at a diner so that we could all grab some goodies to take with us for our long wait. And we would still be the first in line! The three of us would sit together, eating, talking, and laughing about all sorts of things. We thought it was a great time.

When it became clear that Carin and I were going to be great friends, Dad would treat the two of us to ice cream cones once a week. We'd go up the street to the nearby ice cream shop and tell us to help ourselves to whatever we'd like. I still remember my order: A cone with sprinkles. I'd change up the ice cream flavor, depending on my mood. It cost 42 cents. Carin and I felt like we were being spoiled rotten. On top of that, our dads would take turns driving us to the roller rink every Saturday. It was a 20-mile trip, but my dad or Carin's dad would let us stay there the whole day. They would drop us off with some money for snacks and come back to pick us up when it was time to go home. It was so nice to be able to share those memories with someone in the neighborhood.

After our family had moved a bit further away from Amy, it was so nice to have another close friend to play with in Carin. She was so sweet and spunky. I think you'd have to be that way to feel comfortable enough approaching complete strangers and asking to pet their dog. But she wasn't one of those overwhelming, in-your-face-all-the-time kind of personalities, either. She was a lot of fun and had such an active imagination. We made so many memories together just playing outside or doing other simple things. Sometimes, Carin's mom would spend the whole day making Swedish buns that Carin and I would enjoy eating. It was always such a special treat. It was so hard to wait for them to bake, watching the buns rise as the kitchen smelled like fresh bread. It was worth the wait, though; they were so delicious. It didn't take much to entertain us, and we absolutely loved being together.

That's another thing I've always loved about pets: They bring people together. Sure, not everyone is an animal lover, but those who are can't help but want to admire them. There's a good chance that I never would've met Carin if it hadn't been for Tucker since I was at school all day and doing chores or homework all night. But Tucker gave me an outlet to see a little more of my corner of the world and meet some fantastic people along the way.

Not only that, but Tucker himself was one of my closest friends. He provided amazing companionship to me in both the good times and the bad. I could come to him in any mood, and he would always be right there to mirror whatever I was feeling. I was always a bit sad to leave him in the morning and looked forward to seeing him when I got home from school each day.

That's what made it so shocking when he disappeared.

It happened about a year after getting Tucker. I had gone about my daily routine and had finished getting my knuckles beaten in my piano lesson. I was in a lot of pain and really looking forward to coming home and seeing Tucker. But when I arrived, I didn't hear the usual noise he made when he ran to the door.

"Tucker!" I poked my head around the house to see if he was hiding under anything. No response.

"Tucker? Where are you, boy?" I searched and searched for him, looking under all the furniture, but I couldn't find him anywhere. Now I was starting to get worried. *Where could he be?* I thought. *He's never this quiet for this long.*

After a while, I saw my mother at home and thought she might know about it.

"Mom, do you know where Tucker is?" I asked.

A rare look of apparent concern came over her face, which I wasn't used to seeing. She turned her head toward me, but her body stayed oriented in the other direction. What she said next felt like the worst possible news.

"Oh, Emma, he's gone."

Pardon me?

"He needed to go live somewhere where he had more room to roam," she explained. "A nice man came by earlier today to pick him up and take him to his farm a couple of hours away. Oh, don't start crying about this. You'll understand one day."

I didn't.

I couldn't.

How could she do this to me without telling me? What possible explanation could justify such a horrible decision? There was no discussion; there wasn't even a hint that he was being crammed into our supposedly small city life. The best option was just a sudden, 180-degree shift—one day, he was here and happy, and then he was gone the next. I'm sure we could've figured out an arrangement, but she left me no opportunity to present a case for that. It felt like a massive betrayal.

I was devastated, to say the least. I cried for weeks. It took me years to get over it. I still think about Tucker to this day, especially when I see another dog that looks like him. What an absolutely horrible thing to do to a child.

Now, I'm going to jump ahead in the narrative for a bit, but I'll come back to this point by the end of the chapter. There's something else you need to know about this story.

Tucker didn't really go to a farm with a nice man that day.

The truth about Tucker came out many years later. I was having a conversation with my mom on any average day about nothing in particular when the topic of Tucker eventually came up.

"Hey, Mom, do you remember Tucker?" I asked her.

"Tucker... Oh, the dog? Sure, sure," she responded.

"Man, I loved that dog. He was great. I missed him so much when he went away."

My mom's eyebrows shot up. I don't really remember what we were talking about before that moment, but her tune certainly changed with that comment.

"Oh, yeah... I never did tell you what really happened, did I?"

I immediately perked my head up toward her. "What do you mean, 'what really happened'? Did he not go to the farm?"

She started to chuckle. "Oh, yeah, wow, I forgot I told you that! No, he wasn't even close to a farm. At least, not the last time I saw him. I'd just met some guy from East Hartford who was gettin' robbed a lot, and he was looking to get a watchdog to stop it. I figured, 'Hey, we have a dog,' so I just gave it to him."

She was starting to build more laughter into her speech now.

"And I thought, wouldn't it be so funny to see you come back home all nervous about where he is, only to find out he was gone? And you did! You were so worried, like, 'Oh no, where's the dog? Where's the dog?' Meanwhile, he was out in some junkyard barking off robbers in East Hartford! Oh, I had such a good time with that. You should've seen the look on your face. I couldn't bring myself to tell you the full truth, so I figured I'd just tell you a nice story so that this whole thing would blow over, and you'd know that he was in a better place. It's so great to be past that now."

First of all, speak for yourself.

Second of all, the *full* truth? How about *any* of it?!

How on earth she thought this was all okay is beyond me. Don't ask me how she ever met this guy or what made the two of them think that Tucker was any kind of watchdog because I have no idea, and he was far from that.

It gets worse.

"Oh, I guess that means I didn't tell you what happened after that, either," she added.

I just stared at her, seething with rage.

"Well, about a week after he got there," she began, already laughing, "the junkyard was robbed again! I guess that mutt wasn't good for much because the robbers ended up taking him with all the other stuff. Some watchdog, huh?"

It almost didn't feel real. I couldn't comprehend how someone could feel so comfortable and even at ease talking about something so cruel. She treated it as though it was an ordinary piece of information; if anything made it extraordinary, it was in how hilarious it was. In reality, there couldn't be anything further from the truth.

All these years later, it still hurts so badly to replay her words in my mind. She knew how much I loved that dog, but because it was an inconvenience to her, she had no problem sending it away. The end justified the means; in other words, as long as she got her way, she could do whatever she felt needed to be done to arrive at her desired conclusion.

I later realized this became a precedent for what happened a few decades later, but I won't get too far ahead of myself just yet. Up to this point in my life, losing Tucker in such a terrible fashion was the most heartbreaking event that had happened to me. There was nothing in my mind that could replace him.

Pets energize the home in a way no human can; even the quietest fish still adds character to its environment. They're a lot of work, but they bring so much joy that makes the hard work worth it. I would've taken several more years of hard work with Tucker if that meant I got to have him back. I never had closure with him. I didn't get to mourn when he was taken away from me properly, and it has left my heart a bit broken ever since.

But as devastating as it was to find out that Tucker was gone, it still wasn't as surprising as coming home to find my mother with a man who wasn't my father.

Chapter 5:

Stay out of the Kitchen

It happened during summer vacation.

I was playing outside one day with a few neighborhood friends, making the most of the free time I had to play instead of doing homework. Connecticut isn't typically warm for most of the year, so when the summer months roll around, the locals love to make the most of it. I loved to spend as much time outside as possible. Even the rainy days were considered potential playing days; running around and getting messy with friends was just fun. That's what we did back then.

But on this particular day, my friends and I were enjoying the beautiful sunshine and having a grand old time together. After some time had passed, I needed to go back to my house for something. I don't remember what it was now, but it doesn't make a difference to this story. But I had to go back for it, and my friends and I were a bit further down the street. Our house was still close enough that I could quickly run back to my place, grab the thing I needed, and be back with my friends within the span of a couple of minutes. No problem.

So, I ran over to my house and just let myself in. The door was unlocked, so I figured my mom was around doing some kind of cleaning or cooking. It was a lot quieter than I'd expected it to be, though, but I didn't think much of it until I went further inside.

The first thing I noticed was the rancid smell of room-temperature beer. It lingered across the entire main floor. It made me want to puke. Of course, I couldn't have avoided the smell if I wanted to, so I just held my breath as best I could.

As I stood there, I thought I might've heard stirring in the kitchen. I noticed that there was a pair of shoes I didn't recognize by the front door, so I wondered if there was someone over who wasn't supposed to be. I had my reasons to be on guard for robbers.

As I inched closer to the kitchen, I was getting more and more anxious. Empty beer bottles were strewn all over our kitchen table and onto the floor. *Well, maybe Mom's having company over,* I thought. *Both me and Dad are out, so maybe she's just enjoying herself.*

Then, I saw my mom in there with her friend's husband, kissing each other as she sat on his lap.

My eyes widened to be as large as dinner plates. I couldn't believe what I was seeing. I must've let out a slight gasp because my mom raised her head to see me staring directly at her.

"What are you doing here?!" she yelled at me. "Get back outside, and don't come in unless I tell you to! Get out!"

I turned around in a panic and ran back out as fast as I could. I never ended up getting what I'd intended to grab when I came back inside. I just ran as quickly as my legs would move me, trying to burn off the surge of adrenaline that rushed through my body. I'd fully entered "flight" mode and wanted to get the heck out of there.

My heart thundered in my chest, and my face was frozen for several minutes. I don't think I was capable of lowering my eyebrows at that moment. I went back to playing with my friends, but I was so rattled by everything that I couldn't concentrate on whatever game we'd been playing. I was stunned. What had I just witnessed?

I delayed coming home for as long as I could that day, but I knew I had to eat eventually. When the time inevitably came, I carefully opened and closed the front door, making as much noise as possible without causing a scene. I wanted everyone to know that I was home. And now, I knew better than to just run freely around the house.

I started kicking off my shoes at the front door when Dad walked over to greet me.

"Hey, sweetie. How was it with your friends?" he asked with a smile.

"Good." I didn't mean to come across as blunt, but I was so horrified about where my mother might be that I didn't know how to respond.

"Well, I'm glad you had fun," he said. "Mom's just finishing up dinner. We'll be eating in a few minutes if you want to start washing up."

I nodded as I shuffled my way toward the kitchen. The beer bottles were nowhere to be found and the smell was mostly covered up by our dinner. I poked my head in to see my mother cooking something on the stovetop. I knew that she knew I was home, but she didn't look at me. I'd never seen her more intensely focused on stirring whatever was in the frying pan. Honestly, I was fine with that. I much preferred that to the alternative of having to acknowledge what had happened earlier.

I decided that I'd wash my hands in the bathroom.

Neither my mom nor I ever spoke about that day again.

That moment was burned into my memory from that day onward. I wished that I could get that horrible image out of my head, but the damage had been done. It scarred me. No kid ever wants to see their parents doing any kind of "adult" stuff in the first place, never mind with another man or woman. I didn't know much about the guy, but I did know that he had his own family, and he certainly wasn't my father. I felt sick to my stomach just thinking about it. If I'd been holding onto any hope that my parents were happy together, that was shattered after that experience.

But the worst part about the whole affair wasn't the actual image of my mother with someone else. It was imagining the hurt that Dad would've experienced if he ever found out about it.

I desperately wanted to tell Dad what I'd seen. I thought about doing it so many times. I wanted him to know because he did not deserve to be treated like that at all. He was the most loyal husband a woman could ever ask for, even when his wife had been so brutal and unappreciative toward him. But not only did she not show him much love or affection, but there were times when I wondered if she was actually rooting against him and wanted to see him fail.

My mom would pick these horrific fights with my dad over the stupidest things. She was the queen of taking non-issues and turning them into massive problems, and he just had to suck it up and take it. And it would be one thing if she was just prone to striking up petty arguments, but if she didn't feel that her rage had been satisfactorily handled, she could get violent.

One morning, Dad was getting ready for work as my mother and I were in the kitchen. As I drank my Carnation breakfast, I noticed my mother's hand clutching the handle of our Pyrex coffee pot while it warmed up on the stovetop. I could barely see the blue flowers on the white pot as she wrapped her fingers around it. She turned her eyes into daggers facing the front door. I didn't know what she was thinking, but this also wasn't a new look for her. I figured she had pushed another argument onto him last night or this morning and was still working through it.

Dad came into the room to say goodbye before grabbing his things and walking out the front door. As he left, my mom hurled the coffee pot—which was full of hot coffee—directly at the door.

SMASH.

The glass made an explosive sound as it blasted against the door. Remnants of our coffee pot scattered everywhere. Coffee and grounds covered our entire front hallway. It was a mess.

I just stared at the door, absolutely stunned. My neck and shoulders had never been so tense. *I have got to spend less time in this kitchen,* I thought to myself. *Nothing good ever seems to happen when I'm here.*

Without missing a beat, my mother turned to me to give me my next set of instructions.

"Clean this up. You're gonna be late for school."

And she walked away.

I must've cleaned it up, but I was in such a state of shock that I probably blocked out the next few moments. It was like the first part of *Cinderella* when her wicked stepmother kept ordering her to do things, except this was my biological mother getting me to do her literal dirty work. I'm just glad I didn't get cut by all the little pieces of glass that had spread across our front hallway.

That doesn't even begin to scratch the surface of the fights my mom would initiate.

During another one of these morning fights, she kept screaming about how she didn't want to have to deal with me.

"Take her to work yourself!" she shouted at Dad. "You never take on any of the responsibilities of looking after her, and I have to do it all myself" (which was an absolute lie, by the way). "I'm not watching over her anymore. You take her."

I had nothing to do with whatever they were arguing about, but she'd regularly use me as a pawn to get what she wanted. Thinking back now, that might've been a way for her to get rid of me so that there'd be an empty house and she could have her friend's husband over again.

I just felt so sorry for Dad. He wasn't allowed to take anyone to work with him for safety reasons, especially a kid. But my mother was determined to get her way, and he didn't think it was worth fighting back.

Once all the yelling had subsided, Dad walked up to my room and knocked lightly on my bedroom door. "Hey, kiddo. How'd you feel about coming to work with me today?"

I always liked spending time with Dad, so I agreed to go, pretending not to hear what my mother had been yelling about.

It ended up being a pretty exciting day for me—I loved being in the truck with Dad and seeing what he did for a living. Once I climbed into the dump truck with him, I had to lay on the floor until we pulled out of the facility so no one would see me. It was cool to observe how he'd control everything from the driving to the lifting, noticing just how precise he had to be with everything. I also distinctly remember the cup of chocolate ice cream we had after lunch while sitting in his truck. It was special to have that time with my dad, although I felt weird knowing how this whole day came about in the first place.

I could go on and on about the fights the two of them would have, but I don't want to belabor the point. She always needed to have the upper hand and feel like she was in control of everything. She had to be the one to make the first move and squash any potential threat to her status before anyone had the chance to usurp her. If there was any chance that someone had more power than her, my mother would shut that down right away.

Hence, when I walked in on her and that other man, she never addressed it afterward. She knew that I had information that could disrupt her entire life and couldn't do anything about it. I think that caused her to take out even more of her anger onto me. While I wanted her to have her comeuppance, I didn't know what the fallout of that action would have on my dad.

It broke my heart to think about what would've happened if he'd ever found out about the affair. On the one hand, I felt that he had a right to know, but on the other hand, I didn't know how much I was allowed to say. It shouldn't be a child's place to get involved in any husband-wife matters, but I was trapped. I knew too much, and I hated it. Our family even went to the man's house on occasion since my mom was friends with his wife. I would play with his two sons while the adults socialized. It was terribly awkward for me. The affair had put me in such a strained position, and I didn't know what to say or who to say it to.

Ultimately, I never said anything to my dad. Even though I'd seriously contemplated doing it, I knew the repercussions would be severe. My mother would never let me hear the end of it, and I worried for my own safety. So, I kept it to myself.

I was still a kid during our years in Hartford, but I was old enough to start forming more vivid, concrete memories of my childhood. Some of these memories might not be as detailed at this point in my life, but the emotions associated with them are incredibly raw. This is especially true concerning my relationship with each of my parents. As I looked back on my Enfield and Hartford years, I discovered how the memories I had formed regarding my parents were viewed through a particular lens.

When it came to my dad, my memories involved the things he did *with* me. I associate all of those memories with such warm, positive emotions. From eating my Easy Bake Oven treats to going for walks with Tucker and me, Dad put in so much effort to let me know that he loved me. I never once questioned his loyalty to me or his desire to see me succeed in all areas of life. I have such fond memories of him from my younger years that were crucial for my development later in life, too.

But when it came to my mom, my memories involved the things she did *to* me. I didn't realize until much later how few memories I had of doing anything fun with my mother as a child. All I could think about were the ways in which she scolded, dismissed, mocked, betrayed, and lied to me. I tried so hard to think of something the two of us had done together, but nothing had ever been seen through. She'd start "brushing" my hair and then send me off to Grandma Joan. She'd start the dishes and then force me to be the one to burn my hands doing it.

She shirked all responsibility as soon as something became slightly inconvenient for her and blamed me whenever she could. As a result, I didn't feel like I had much of a mom at all.

In summary, my mom would be the one to yell at me to do my homework (and hers), while my dad would sit down next to me and help me do it.

But I remained hopeful that the next chapter of my life would change things for the better. Perhaps a change of scenery outside of Connecticut would be the impetus to set things on a better path for our family.

It didn't.

Auburn, Maine

Chapter 6:

The Girls of Summer

I hope I'm not suggesting that my early years were riddled with doom and gloom because there were quite a few highlights from my youth as well.

For instance, do you remember Rose and Jim? They're Amy's parents, who befriended my parents when Amy and I met in Enfield as toddlers. Well, about three years after we moved away from Enfield, my parents, along with Rose and Jim, bought adjacent properties in Auburn together. Our families would make frequent trips to Auburn, coordinating specific dates to make sure that we would be there at the same time. And, as they say, the rest is history.

The trips to Auburn turned out to be a huge part of both Amy's and my childhood. If it turned out that Amy and I spent more time there than we did at our permanent homes, it wouldn't surprise me. Both families would spend weekends and holidays at our Auburn properties, and Amy and I spent the bulk of our summer vacations there, too. We couldn't wait to go to Auburn because it represented a place with no responsibilities, homework, or general stress. Instead, we could just put those issues aside and focus on spending time with each other. Those trips made for a wonderful childhood memory, and I loved how they helped bring our families together.

It really was a stunning property. My family and Amy's family had individual trailers that allowed each of us some privacy, but they were still located right beside each other. That said, what really drew us to the property was the natural beauty surrounding it. There was a river in the front, mountains in the back, and a cow pasture next to us. We were really quite spoiled with various types of landscapes all around us; we could simply turn our heads and see a totally different element of nature.

Another one of the benefits of being surrounded by so much nature was that it allowed us to participate in a number of different activities.

In the summer, Amy and I learned how to swim in that river, and in the winter, we learned how to ice skate on it as well as ski in the mountains behind us. There was a ski lodge right down the road, so we could make frequent trips there and get proper instructions. After living in the city all week, it really felt like our own private retreat center. There was never a shortage of things to do between organized and spontaneous activities, and for a couple of kids, it was an absolute dream.

In the very early years, there was no running water. We took baths in the river (only in the summer, of course) that ran in front of our properties. I remember us washing our hair with Prell shampoo, which is a well-known brand whose shampoo is almost neon green in color. It looked a bit like slime. We'd only ever used ivory soap because that was the only soap that floated, so we thought this was the coolest thing ever. Each property had its own water pump that we'd use for drinking, cooking, and cleaning. There was also an outhouse that we'd use for other bodily functions. It's almost hard to imagine a property like that nowadays, but back then, we made it work. It certainly wasn't how I wanted to do things forever, but it added to the retreat-like experience of being separated from the city. It disconnected us even further from our usual way of doing things which felt like a breath of fresh air (once you left the outhouse).

That being said, it was still an adjustment to get used to a property that didn't have running water inside when the seasons changed. On one particular Thanksgiving, it had already snowed in Maine by the time we had gone up to the property. That isn't necessarily uncommon for Maine, but it definitely made for an interesting challenge when it came to using well water. The water had been frozen for a while, and we were a bit puzzled as we tried to figure out how to melt frozen water in the early days of winter. We ended up going outside, filling pots with snow, and heating it on the stove so that we could wash the dishes. The wind and snow felt like pins and needles against our skin as we alternated between going outside in the cold and coming back into the warmth. It was frigid out there, but we found the whole thing exhilarating.

I often wished that my children could've had the same experience with a summer home or second property. It was truly such a wonderful reprieve from the day-to-day monotony of life that can weigh on all of us at times. When we were surrounded by beautiful scenery and far removed from our home base, it gave us a chance to simply breathe and remember what really matters in life. I would've loved to have shared that with my kids, but we found other ways of having that quality family time. For me and Amy, quality time together meant going outside as much as possible.

We also didn't have a television in Auburn like we did at home, which forced us kids to run around a whole lot. Amy and I would play tag with our friends who lived in Auburn year-round for hours. We'd go well into the dark almost every night, but it was such a safe environment that I don't think our parents were ever too worried about us. The kids never grew tired of it, which is why I wanted my kids to have an experience like that, too. It was an opportunity to make a whole new group of friends while not even having the option of sitting in front of a screen all day. We didn't even miss the TV when we were up there because we were way too excited to play games with our friends.

In this day and age, with technology being what it is, it feels increasingly more difficult to separate ourselves from screens of any kind. Seeing young kids absorbed in their phones makes me especially sad because I remember the fond times I had going outside and just being a kid. They shouldn't have to worry about grown-up matters they're now exposed to on their phones. I believe putting them down or turning off the computer and TV screens is so important, and spending an uninterrupted amount of time in the great outdoors is way more rejuvenating. I'm so thankful I had these years at the Auburn property, and I just hope that kids these days can have something similar.

But it wasn't just the river and mountains that we made use of while we were in Auburn. Amy and I would often visit the farm just down the road as well. We soon became friends with Keith, the boy who lived on the farm and often played our games of tag on that property. Sometimes, Amy and I would go up to the hayloft, lay on the hay bales, and talk there for hours. We felt like we were in our own little world, talking about life and staring at the ground below us. It was so peaceful up there.

One of the special parts about going to the farm would be visiting all the animals. I've always had a fondness for them, and after the whole fiasco with Tucker had happened, it was nice to see all sorts of animals again. It was really neat when we'd go during the birthing season, and we actually got to see calves being born. We would always try to get down there at night when it was time for milking the cows. We weren't grossed out by it; we found it fascinating. But one of my favorite animals, without a doubt, had to be Tico, the pony.

Tico lived on a horse farm about ten miles away from our property and was the sweetest of creatures. Amy and I adored him so much that our fathers would occasionally bring him to our place so that we could ride him. Dad and Jim would drive together to Tico's farm, and then one dad would drive back at two miles per hour while the other dad sat in the trunk holding Tico's reins. That was how "fancy" our families were. It was a sight for sore eyes. Tico was so obedient as he calmly walked behind the car. He never got fussy and always behaved so well for all of us. We circled our properties hundreds of times with him without any issues. He was the gentlest pony.

How many dads do you know who would do that over and over again for their kids? I got a much greater appreciation for the sacrifice involved in being a parent when I became one myself, but our dads certainly laid the groundwork for that. A loving parent would want to move the ends of the earth just to see their kid smile. While I don't think I ever took that for granted with my dad, I didn't realize just how much he did for me until much later in life. He only wanted the best for me, and I adored him for that.

In addition to Tico, our other great ride came in the form of a 1960 blue Chevy Corvair. It was Grandpa Walter's car that he was planning on taking to the junkyard. It was all ready to go, but he decided to give it to Amy instead to practice driving. For context, we were 12 years old at the time. You could imagine how excited we were to play with—I mean, drive-in—an actual car at that age!

Don't worry; our parents were responsible when it came to letting us drive. The Corvair had a push-button shifter on the dashboard, which, from our perspective, just meant that we had a bunch of buttons to push (before we were promptly told which ones we absolutely could *not* push). Amy and I were only allowed to go up and down the driveway with the car. We'd take turns backing down the 100-foot grass driveway and then driving back to the top again. We would do this for hours, to the point where there were sizable ruts in the driveway when we were done.

We perfected the art of backing up at a young age, which made things a bit easier when Dad taught me how to drive properly a few years later. I was already a seasoned pro at reversing, although he endured many complaints from me when it came to taking driving directions from him. But he stuck with me and remained patient through it all. Even in my older years, he wouldn't hesitate to drive me to work if it was snowing. This was after he had worked all night on the third shift, but because he knew I didn't like driving in the snow, he'd do it anyway.

But going back to this story, our Corvair wasn't the only nice car in the neighborhood. We had a wonderful neighbor down the road from us named Leo, an older man who quickly became a friend of ours. He would drive up to his property for a weekend getaway from Ossipee, New Hampshire, about an hour and a half away. He made the trek in his Subaru with his four barking Rottweilers.

Every time he came up, he would always bring us pastries from Ossipee. Amy and I would always look forward to that. There are few joys that are quite as delicious as small-town desserts. We would go to Leo's house to play different games, but the one we played the most often was Clue. He was always Colonel Mustard. I'm not sure why; perhaps Leo liked the sophisticated military man out of the bunch. There were so, so many great memories with him, and he was an integral part of my experience there.

It was a sad day when Leo died. A very sad day. It felt like we were losing a family member of our own. This happened many years after our families had stopped going to Auburn, but hearing the news brought me right back to the pastries and Colonel Mustard days.

Leo always made it known that he wanted us to find homes for his dogs after he died. Being the animal lover that I am, I sought to find safe and happy dwellings for his Rottweilers with my husband. We found places for two of them, and Rose found a home for the third. The fourth dog, Stormi, was our favorite, so my husband and I ended up keeping her for ourselves. She was a big, beautiful girl and brought so much joy to our family.

During the early summer period, Amy and I would enjoy long days and nights together without a care in the world. For the adults, though, the world still had to carry on. Dad and Jim would have to work back at home during the week while my mother and Rose would stay in Auburn with the kids. Once us kids had gone to bed, the moms had their version of fun.

Amy and I would be trying to sleep, but we couldn't always go to sleep right away. When our mothers thought we were long gone, they would make their way to the bathroom and start chatting with a more "adult" tone of voice. Amy and I could hear them putting on makeup and spraying their hair, getting ready for a night on the town. We didn't know exactly where they were planning on going, but it didn't sound like a kid-friendly place. We'd hear them slip out the front door at night and be asleep by the time morning came around.

When Amy and I would come out for breakfast, we'd see our mothers in the kitchen looking a bit tired. We didn't hide the fact that we were awake.

"Where did you go last night?" one of us would ask.

My mother and Rose would give each other a quick glance before one of them would respond, "We just went out for coffee."

It was the same story every time. We knew it wasn't true. To this day, I still don't know if the dads ever knew that their wives were hitting the town doing who-knows-what while they were at home working. And honestly, that's one sneaking suspicion that I don't want to know the answer to.

So, my parents were still my parents, with my dad helping me take pony rides during the limited time he had with me and my mom ditching me the first chance she got. But on the whole, Auburn meant so much joy and excitement that I looked forward to going there as often as I could. It was so nice to stay in touch with Amy so easily, which probably played a huge role in our enduring friendship. We matured a lot during that time, both physically and emotionally. Auburn was very much a coming-of-age town for us that was about to become even more significant.

After several years of traveling back and forth from Connecticut to Maine, my parents decided to move to Auburn permanently. I was going into the ninth grade at the time, which meant that I would be starting high school in a new state. It was a good time to transition into a new environment since I was just finishing up elementary school and would have to attend a new school anyway.

Even though we had to leave Hartford, I always remained friends with Carin. As I write this book, it has been about 45 years since she first approached me and Dad asking to pet Tucker. It has been a wonderful friendship, and I look forward to making many more memories with her in the years to come.

Unfortunately, a different friendship I had made in the Auburn years caused my mother to make one of her most irrational decisions yet.

Chapter 7:

Teenage Dreams and Nightmares

It was a big change for me to go from a Catholic school to a public one.

Sure, I'd gone to public school for kindergarten, but that was ages ago. I didn't really know what to expect starting a new school in a new state in a public school. I mean, I expected the clothing to be different, and that was definitely one of the changes I observed. It was great not to have to wear a uniform to school every day and face the wrath of the nuns. It still unnerves me to think about what they'd punish me for, depending on how much skin they saw on my body and how bad their mood was on any given day. But other than that, I couldn't remember what it was like to be in a public school.

Turns out, it's way more relaxed. At least, it was that way in my high school. It was a total contrast from my last one in terms of the treatment I received from my teachers. Believe it or not, hitting students on the knuckles every time they made a mistake wasn't the norm! Can you imagine?

I was delightfully surprised to see that teachers and students, by and large, treated each other with dignity and respect. Teachers would give their students instructions without having to screech at them, and the students simply did what they were told. Any outliers to that standard usually deserved whatever punishment they received, to be honest. And while we all had our favorite and least favorite teachers, pretty much everyone there was a decent human being who wanted their students to succeed. What a welcome surprise.

But the biggest shock I experienced during the transition was the level of material being taught, in that I already knew a lot of it. Everything we were learning in math class was something I had already learned at the Catholic school. Because of that, ninth-grade math was a breeze for me. Don't get me wrong; I still wished that I could've spent more of my elementary years playing with my friends, especially if I'd known that I would've been learning this stuff in a couple of years anyway. But if there was any benefit to being cooped up inside doing chores and homework all day, it's that it gave me a lot more freedom and mental capacity to enjoy myself during high school.

My high school years were the first time I can remember actually having fun in some of my classes. It helped that I didn't have to take all the standard courses that were necessary in elementary school. They were all fine, but I was stressed out the entire time. But now, I got to play games other than dodgeball and cook in school! If this was what it meant to grow up, then I couldn't wait to see what other courses were in store.

Out of all of the classes I took, I especially loved Spanish class. It was neat to learn a new language and all, but my classmates and I got to know each other really well. We had a smaller class since Spanish is an elective course that isn't a requirement for many college programs, so it was a really laid-back environment. It was so much fun to explore my own creativity in ways other than writing a poem or drawing a house, too.

I'm a big advocate for those classes today because they helped me learn valuable skills outside of academic or professional contexts. I loved having the chance to use other parts of my brain and my body that wasn't offered in science labs or geographical maps. Those classes are still incredibly valuable, and I'm not saying that we shouldn't take them. But it saddens me sometimes to think about how kids totally immerse themselves in those subjects without exploring more artistic or kinesthetic classes. I loved the hands-on skills I learned in those classes, which served me well outside of high school. Plus, they also helped me develop social skills that I could apply in many types of relationships.

But, of course, there's more to adolescence than the academic side of things. While I was in Auburn, both before and after our permanent move, I delved into the complicated and exhilarating world of puberty and teenagers. Thankfully, that wonderfully awkward and complicated period of life is made much easier by having my best friend around all the time. Since Amy and I were together so often, we shared a lot of our "firsts" together. Our first dates, first kisses, first boyfriends, first proms… All of that happened in Auburn. We even had our own memorable place that we called "The Point," but I think I will leave it at that.

Amy and I would talk for hours about our various experiences with boys, talking about who we thought was cute or who might have a crush on us. That would lead to us discussing how we felt about them and if we'd consider going on a date with them, and subsequently, how those dates went. We had our hearts broken and put back together again a few times, hugging one another through every stage of the process. But no matter what boy came and went in our lives, our bond with each other was still the strongest one I had with any of my peers during my teenage years. Her friendship always remained one of my prized possessions that I cherished above all else.

Our first experience going on a date was actually a double date with two guys. It definitely helped ease the nerves of dating for the first time, knowing that Amy was there and we could make sure we were both okay. We were both so excited and nervous at the same time and kept sneaking little glances at each other throughout the whole date.

It ended up being a lot of fun. The boys pushed us around in grocery store carts all the way to the movie theater. We knew we were in for a fun time at that point. At the theater, we all went to see *Easy Rider*, which was par for the course since our dates were very much into motorcycles. Later on, they took Amy and me for rides on their motorcycles, which would've probably terrified my father if he knew the extent of that. But he did know some stuff because Amy and I would go to their motor cross races and come home covered in dirt. It's pretty hard to explain why two teenage girls would come home so filthy without some kind of vehicle stirring up all kinds of mud and dust.

On top of experiencing these changes for myself, my parents also had to adapt as their daughter was maturing into a young woman. Dad would take me shopping for school clothes, which was a new experience for me—not because of Dad, but the clothes themselves. Other than picking which version of the school uniform to wear on a given day, I'd never had much of a choice when it came to school clothing.

Bless his heart; my dad did the best he could. I mean, most fathers I know don't exactly have a keen eye for teenage girls' fashion, especially before the Internet. He would walk around the store with me and try to pick out things that he thought I might like and to be fair, his choices weren't terrible. When I went to try them on, he'd offer his feedback, although 99% of the time, he'd say the same thing.

"That looks great, sweetie. Do you like it?"

He was a supportive dad from the start, even when he wasn't exactly sure what he was supporting.

My mother, on the other hand, wasn't exactly helpful when I started going through my womanly transitions. When I had to start wearing a bra, she'd just hand me the first one she found off the rack and say, "Here, wear this." Forget about sizing, material, or style—she just wanted to buy something that mostly fit and get the heck out of there. I don't know if she was bored or uncomfortable by the whole thing, but it made me feel like I was wasting her time. I'd try something on in a hurry, and it wouldn't feel right, but I could sense her impatience through the changing room doors. I'd feel pressured just to buy it and go so I wouldn't set her off in the store. Only afterward would I have to learn how to buy stuff for myself because she wouldn't help me in that area.

It was the same way in other areas of my life, too. While we were at home one day, she came into my room and handed me a book.

"Read this," she said.

I looked at the title: *All About Getting Your First Period.*

Oh, yippee.

She had me read about everything myself instead of taking the time to personally explain what happens during that time of the month. While I liked being able to process that information on my own time, it would've been really helpful to see a demonstration of how to use pads and tampons. But since she didn't want to help me through that "period" (pun intended), I didn't want to go the extra mile to tell her more than I had to. I was way more comfortable talking to Amy about that kind of stuff than I was with her, anyway.

Most teenage girls may put up a front that they want to mature into a woman, but that first bra shopping trip and that first period are often awkward or stressful experiences. Girls have never gone through it before, and it feels embarrassing to talk about. A lot of girls feel insecure about their chest being either "too big" or "too small" compared to that of their peers. Plus, it's not easy to figure out which combination of numbers and letters is the best fit for their bodies. On the other hand, periods just show up one day, and nothing really prepares girls for that moment. In a panic, they yell out to their moms for help, with their mothers standing outside the bathroom door and guiding them through the process. Friends are helpful, but they're still figuring it all out, too. Mothers are the ones who are supposed to have the most wisdom to pass on to their girls. And although I knew my mom had that, she didn't seem willing to share it with me.

Something else I really appreciated about Dad was how he made an effort to get to know my friends. He knew Amy and Carin really well, but even in the transient teen years, where friends come and go a bit more easily, he'd always be willing to say hi when they'd drop in. Once my friends and I were concert-going age, he'd be the one to drive us to the shows and wait outside for us. He always made sure that he was on time, and we never had to wait for him to show up. My friends were all really comfortable with him, and they were grateful that he'd be willing to drive them with me. They'd say things to me like, "Oh, your dad's so sweet! He's so involved in everything." And they were right.

They said different things about my mom.

It didn't help that she didn't put in any effort to get to know any of my friends. Instead of asking them questions or having a pleasant conversation with them, she'd find a way to try to mock me about my ability to form meaningful relationships. For instance, any time I made a new girlfriend or spent a lot of time with a certain friend, she'd smirk, roll her eyes, and ask me, "So what, are you a lesbian or something?"

In her mind, I guess I just wasn't allowed to have friends of any kind without there being something wrong with me or them or both. My friends would call her "Mommie Dearest" in reference to that movie about Joan Crawford. I can't lie; I thought it was pretty clever. And, at times, accurate.

But even my friends, with their limited understanding of my family dynamics, could sense that something was seriously off between my parents. Dad was the kindest man who was interested in learning more about these people because they were important to me. It didn't matter if we would drift apart after high school, but as long as they were a part of my life now, that was what he cared about. My mother never even gave them a shot. If anything, she tried to shut down the chance for me to form a meaningful friendship before it had the potential to actually grow into that.

Which brings me to David.

David was a guy I had met in school. We got along really well and became friends over the years. I always thought David was a great person, and I liked talking to him and hanging out with him among our group of friends.

Then, at the end of my junior year, my mother confronted me with some news.

"We're moving back to Connecticut," she said out of the blue.

I was a little thrown off by the remark, but I didn't want to freak out prematurely. "What? Why? This is so random."

"I don't like this David boy you're spending time with."

"What? David? What does he have to do with anything?" I was seriously confused now. "He's just a friend."

"You need to stay away from him. He's not a good influence on you."

"What do you mean? He's a great guy. There's nothing—"

And then it hit me. David was Hispanic.

I had never thought that this was an issue at any point in our friendship. If anything, I found it to be a great opportunity to learn from someone who'd had different experiences from me. Our races didn't matter in forming a wonderful bond. I looked forward to getting to know him and his culture better whenever I saw him. But as soon as my mother found out about him, her response was to relocate to an entirely different state just to get away from him.

Can you imagine doing something so judgmental and drastic? There was nothing to be concerned about at all with the guy. She was just afraid of anything that was different from what she knew, which, in her mind, made it wrong or bad. To this day, I believe that she already knew that she wanted to move back to Connecticut and just used David as an excuse. This was a wildly offensive way to go about it, and I was just horrified.

As an aside, David got in contact with me about 30 years after this incident to catch up. He was married with children and living a few states away. It was wonderful to hear his voice and find out how great he was doing. I just wish we would've had more time to build on that friendship.

Unfortunately, back in high school, my mother was insistent on moving. Before I knew it, our family was getting ready to re-cross state borders and start over once again in Connecticut.

Thank God Amy's parents had something to say about it.

Willington, Connecticut

Chapter 8:

Senior Year

"You can't go to a new school before the start of your senior year!"

Finally. I was glad to hear that some people still have common sense.

When Rose and Jim heard about the situation, they found the reaction to be a bit extreme as well, but they had to be delicate with their reaction. They were best friends with my parents and didn't want to challenge their authority when it came to raising their children. But at the same time, they also didn't think that I should make such a huge move during my last year of high school. Crossing state borders and moving to a new town right before a pretty significant year to that point wasn't something they felt was fair.

They also knew how close I was with Amy, so they came up with a brilliant idea.

"Why don't you come to live with us, Em? That way, you can spend more time with Amy, which will make her so happy. You know all of her friends, anyway. It makes sense to us, and it's no trouble to have you here. What do you say?"

They were stepping in to rescue me. I was all in.

Of course, I couldn't be totally separated from my parents for a full year, so both sets of parents worked out an arrangement. I'd stay at Rose and Jim's house during the week, which was roughly 30 minutes away from my parents' new place, and take the train back to visit my parents on weekends. It would be a lot of commuting, but I was more than willing to pay that price if it meant I didn't have to start all over again with a completely new group of people. I still didn't know most people at the school, but at least I had Amy, so I knew I'd be okay.

I am forever grateful to Rose and Jim for taking me in that year. If I'd gone back to live with my parents, I think I could've let my teenage angst and hormones get the best of me sometimes. I was frustrated but didn't want to be resentful, so it was helpful to have some space. And I'll always be thankful to Amy, too, for basically sharing her whole life with me that year. It takes a lot for a teenage girl to share her private space with someone else, but she embraced me with open arms. As a result, senior year turned into a year-long sleepover with my best friend.

It was such a fun year. Because Amy and I shared a room, it almost felt like we were roommates in a dorm (except that we actually had home-cooked meals and didn't have any bills to pay). The two of us would go to school together during the day, get together with some friends afterward, and stay up talking at night. It was a dream scenario for me. And yes, we still made time to do our homework and all that, but we also made sure that we had our fun in our last year.

My social life was certainly more active during senior year. Living with Amy caused me to spend a lot more time with her other friends outside of school. They were all so welcoming, which allowed me to feel like I fit in so naturally with the group. I should've figured as much—Amy was one of the greatest people I knew, and anyone who'd been friends with her already proved that they had great taste. If they got along with her, then it would make sense that they'd also be warm and inclusive people. Although it's always tough to be the new person in a group, the silver lining was that I got to make a whole new group of friends out of it. I was so grateful for that.

While we were at her house, Amy and I would also have our version of "theme nights" when it came to sharing meals. Basically, we made certain meals on certain days of the week that fit into whatever theme we'd chosen. I remember that Thursday night dinners, in particular, were canned ham and mashed potato nights. I would always be in charge of mashing the potatoes, and I owned that station. It was my favorite meal of the week. Honestly, what's not to love about potatoes, mashed or otherwise?

Those dinners were a blast. It was so much fun to hang out in the kitchen together. Our conversations would alternate between engaging in deep, existential life chats to laughing at our light-hearted kitchen failures. It was a great way to simultaneously learn valuable life skills while also learning to have a great time with food. It may have helped pave the way for my love of cooking and hosting later in life, too.

After dinner, Rose would always leave with her friend Joyce to go to play Pokeno. That would give Amy and me a bit more freedom to do whatever we wanted to do. Sometimes, that involved us being responsible teenagers, and at other times, that involved us being, well, typical teenagers.

One of the best days ever happened when Amy got her first car. A 1967 Chevrolet Bel Air. It was a thing of beauty. It looked like a classic car that someone would think of when they think of '60s vehicles (perhaps I'm biased, but I think it's true). We weren't necessarily thinking about that at the time, though. Sure, it helped that it was pretty, but what made it especially appealing was that it had four round wheels and an engine to take us places. Cars meant freedom, and we were stoked to have more of that.

Amy getting a car meant she could now drive the two of us to school every day, which was a new experience for me. I definitely appreciated the reprieve of driving to a relaxed school environment instead of walking three miles to a much stricter one. But, of course, when you're the kid who has a car, everyone else wants to get in on the action. It's like being that person who opens a pack of gum and is immediately obligated to give a piece to everyone else who happens to be around at that time but on a larger scale.

Amy and I would pick up several people on our way to school, and we'd cram as many bodies into that vehicle as we could possibly manage. I'm pretty sure there were some days when I would barely be sitting on a seat because there were so many other people in there. Seat belt laws were much more lax back then. On top of that, every time we got into the car, it felt like "Hotel California" by the Eagles would be playing on the radio. Naturally, we'd have to sing along. To this day, every time I hear that song, I go right back to those days of squeezing people into Amy's car.

I wouldn't recommend that kids today do what we did, but it definitely captures the spirit of being a teenager. It's that sweet spot of life where you're granted more autonomy than you had as a child, but you don't have full weight of adulthood on your shoulders yet. Of course, teenagers should still be responsible when it comes to their future and setting themselves up as best they can, absolutely. But I worry that a lot of kids these days are letting the joy of their youth slip away in an effort to grow up more quickly than they need to. Teens shouldn't have to worry about the fate of the world. We aren't teenagers for very long, and I don't want kids to miss out on that special time in their life. It's okay to embrace that!

As for me, the biggest concern I had at that point in my life was what to wear to our graduation ball. It was our school's version of an end-of-year celebration for the seniors to acknowledge the end of their high school journey. Amy and I were so excited. And I mean, *so* excited. After waiting for roughly three and a half years, it was finally our turn to get all dressed up in fancy gowns with gorgeous make-up and stylish hair. So, we wanted to go all out for it.

The grad ball theme was kept a secret from the senior class until they arrived that night, so none of us had any idea what we'd be walking into. That also gave us the freedom to dress and style ourselves however we wanted instead of feeling any kind of pressure to match the theme, which was nice. We knew that going shopping for our whole get-up was going to be enough of a thrill on its own. Plus, it was fun to keep guessing at what we thought the theme was going to be. All in all, we expected the "getting ready" part to be just as much fun as the "going out" part. And it was.

Amy and I went to the mall to pick out our dresses. It was a dream come true to wander up and down the aisles, perusing the beautiful gowns and having a legitimate excuse to try them on. When we'd go shopping together in the past, it would always be tempting to try on the nice dresses for fun, and sometimes we did it anyway. But now that we actually had to buy a nice dress, we couldn't wait to get started.

It felt like we were in a movie montage. We'd go into our changing rooms, put on fabulous dresses, and then walk out at the same time. We took turns striking poses for each other while saying how good the other person looked. I'd type out the things we said here, but it looks far too embarrassing in writing. I'm sure the slang we used in those days is highly outdated now. But we had a blast with it. In a way, making the final decision was the least fun part because we didn't have an excuse to keep trying on dresses. Thankfully, we both loved the dresses we eventually settled on.

When the night of the grad ball finally came, Amy and I and all of her friends had a pre-party with our dates. We gushed over how stunning everybody looked in their dresses and took pictures with all the couples. That was all fine and well, but picture time also gave us a chance to get a teensy bit of a buzz and tuck a small flask into our purses before making our way to the school. Let's just say we were feeling especially great heading into the night.

Then, it was time to discover the grad ball theme finally.

We were given a ride to the school, walked into the gym, and discovered a beautiful beach scene. It was a Caribbean-themed event. The gym had been totally transformed with colorful decorations and music to make us feel like we could pull up a chair and lounge under a palm tree. Kudos to the organizing committee who put everything together because they did an incredible job. We were all blown away. Little did we know that this wasn't going to be the last surprise of the night.

All the couples took their seats at their given tables. The buzz was still going pretty strong, and everyone was looking forward to keeping the night going. As our table was starting to settle in, a few waiters visited Amy and me to kick things off.

"Good evening, ladies. We'll be your waiters for the night. May I interest you in some virgin piña coladas this evening?"

Amy and I recognized those voices right away. We looked at each other with wide eyes before looking up to see the servers, and we couldn't believe who was standing above us.

Dad and Jim were decked out in white pants, tropical shirts, and sun hats. They held a tray of drinks in their hands, ready to hand out to their not-so-little, not-so-sober girls.

We were shocked and honestly a little bummed out. We couldn't believe our dads were leaning so heavily into the Caribbean theme and spent the whole night looking like American tourists. Then again, we also weren't expecting to be spending our senior ball with our dads at all. It made for a very interesting reaction from the two of us, who made a careful attempt at hugging our dads without letting them smell our breath. We thought we were being so subtle. I'm almost positive that they could smell the alcohol anyway, but they didn't let it spoil the night for them or for us.

When I think about it now, though, it was such a sweet thing for our dads to do. It means so much more now that I'm a mother, and I understand the love that a parent has for a child. But even while I was still a teenager, I remember that it still meant a lot that my dad had come to visit me. I hadn't been able to see him a whole lot that year, so it was really special to have him see me on a night when I felt so beautiful. I just had to watch my step and make sure I didn't do anything too embarrassing. I miss being able to have those kinds of surprises now, so memories like that mean even more to me.

Senior year was the best year of my life to that point. It was like all of the best parts of being in school mixed with all the best parts of being on summer vacation. I got to meet so many amazing people and have more freedom than ever before while spending so much time with Amy. I was young, somewhat wild and free, just starting to see the world from a new perspective and absolutely loving it.

But while senior year was fantastic, we also couldn't wait to get out of high school and start the next chapter of our lives as adults with even more freedom. The saddest part would be going in separate directions from all these wonderful people. Some of us would stay in contact, and some would lose touch, just like any other social group, but the bonds we established during those teen years were genuine and beautiful. I still think so fondly of them today and hope everyone continues to be well. We shared some great times together.

And I guess the Caribbean theme really left an impression on us because Amy and I and two other friends went to the Cayman Islands for real the following year. It was our first adult adventure after graduation. Don't get me wrong, the high school gym was great for what it was, but wow, it can't begin to compare to the real thing. To this day, I don't know if I've seen bluer water or whiter beaches than I'd seen in the Cayman Islands. It was absolutely stunning, and we had an amazing time.

Since that trip, I've been to the Cayman Islands eight more times. Before starting my family, I'd visit cousins who lived there, and later on, my husband, children, and I just enjoyed a family vacation there together. I've certainly seen it from almost every angle. I've had my fill of the Cayman Islands now, but I'll always hang onto those precious memories.

Speaking of my husband, I suppose this would be a good time to tell you how the two of us got started.

The Next 27 Years

Chapter 9:

The Ride of a Lifetime

Seven years after finishing high school, I met a young man named James.

First impressions are crucial in determining if two people want to keep talking to each other, and that came into play with James. He was a kind, helpful, and hardworking gentleman. He was the go-to guy whenever someone needed something. And the more I looked at him, the faster my heart started beating around him. I desperately tried to "play it cool" as I tried to prevent my cheeks from turning too red around him, if that's even possible. I think I was mostly successful at that. It was enough for me to feel like I could spend more time with him without embarrassing myself.

James was a quieter and friendly man but also a bit spontaneous. I used to love it when he'd just show up somewhere when I wasn't expecting him. One time, I went out with Carin for her birthday, and he knew where we were going. During our meal, he walked into the restaurant with a present for her, said happy birthday to her, and left us to finish our dinner. He was such a good-natured man while still having just the right amount of edginess, too.

It also helped that he had a motorcycle. I'm just now realizing as I'm writing this book that there seems to be a pattern with guys I've dated and owning a motorcycle. Did I have a type after all? I promise that I didn't go looking for that sort of thing...

At any rate, he had a motorcycle. In hindsight, it might look like I had a type, but at the time, James' motorcycle certainly didn't win any brownie points with me.

I remember the first day he showed it to me and had an idea of how we could spend our next date.

"Wanna go for a ride?" he asked. He was so smooth in his delivery that I had to stop myself from swooning.

My eyes widened. "Yeah, for sure." My previous experience riding my date's motorcycle suddenly turned into a great practice run. But riding with this handsome young man was even more of a thrill—no complaints from me.

The two of us hopped on, and I wrapped my hands around his torso. He revved up the engine, told me to "hold on tight," and he got us on the road. Things got off to a decent start as he drove around, making sure I was securely gripped to his body. That's when things took a turn—literally.

SCREECH.

I felt a harsh, jerking motion to the right, which caused my whole body to suddenly lean that way as well.

Then, he sped up aggressively before making the same kind of motion to the left, causing my body to follow suit again.

Then, he slowed down.

Then, he hit the gas as quickly as he could.

Then, he jerked left and right in a snake-like, zigzag pattern.

Things devolved quickly as he continued driving quite erratically. The sudden motions back and forth forced me to grip his torso harder than I had intended to. I hoped I wasn't making him queasy or sore, but my body was all tensed up. I certainly couldn't loosen my grip; otherwise, I'd fall off the seat. My helmet kept smacking into his helmet. I didn't know if it felt better to keep my eyes open or closed, as I tried both. I just kept holding on as tightly as I could. It wasn't a pleasant experience for me at all, and I started to get worried at points.

Is he trying to impress me? I wondered thoughts along those lines to myself as he drove. If that was the case, it didn't work. I just wanted the ride to be over.

After we finished up, he parked the bike and let me hop off the back. My legs were shaking as I tried to stand up again.

"So, whadda you think?" he asked.

I didn't want to lie, but I didn't want to tell him the full truth, either.

"You sure know how to drive that thing," I said. "Thanks for giving me a ride on it, but I should get going now. Thanks again—wait, I just said that. Um, yeah, I'll see ya around."

"Okay, yeah. See you around," he said.

I thanked him as politely as I could and got myself out of there.

I kind of shied away from him after that. If that's what it was going to be like to date this guy, then I didn't want it. I didn't know if the way he rode his motorcycle spoke to something deeper about potentially being a bit reckless that I wasn't a fan of. I liked the thrill of the motorcycle, but I never liked feeling uncomfortable or unsafe. So, I distanced myself from him and didn't talk to him as much afterward.

I'm sure James must've wondered what was happening with me during that time. I didn't know how to communicate my feelings to him properly, but I also wasn't exactly sure how I felt. I liked the guy, and I thought that he liked me too. I just wasn't sure if I could be in a relationship with him.

Soon after that incident, I went on a pre-planned trip with some of my friends. It was a good chance for me to have a lot of distance from James without any pressure to have to interact with him. I got to clear my head for a while with my girls and enjoy being on vacation. And although I certainly got to do that, I still couldn't get him out of my head. The thought of him lingered while I was away because I kept wondering if this was worth pursuing or not.

At the end of our trip, we were set to arrive at Kennedy Airport. The weather was terrible that day, which caused several hours of delays before we finally arrived. As we de-boarded the plane and got ready to grab our things, I saw a familiar face standing in the crowd.

James was waiting for me in the baggage claim area.

I was totally surprised. We hadn't made any plans for James to come pick me up that day. JFK was 50 miles away from his house, and we were many hours later than we were supposed to be. I had no idea how long he had been standing there, and he gave no indication that he had been there for such a long time (which he had been).

After recognizing the situation, my friends had no problem telling me what I should do.

"Go with him!" they urged. "After all that trouble he went through to get here, you have to go. Let us know how it goes."

Having just been on vacation with them, they knew how I was feeling about James in that I wasn't sure what to feel. But when they saw all the effort he made so that he could see me as soon as I got off the plane, they knew there was something promising here. After agreeing to go with him, I said my goodbyes to them and got in James's car.

My heart was racing. The excitement of vacationing and seeing James turned into a palpable silence. I was so nervous to see him; I was totally comfortable with him around, but I had a sense that I'd have to confront some of those feelings.

Before we started driving anywhere, he was the one to break the silence.

"Did you have a good trip?" he asked.

"Yeah, yeah, it was great," I said. "We had a lot of fun."

As I responded, he reached over to open up the glove compartment, took out a beautifully wrapped box, and handed it to me. I timidly took the box from his hand.

"What's this?" I asked.

He stared deeply at me for what felt like an eternity. He thought about how to answer that question before arriving at a suitable response.

"My motorcycle."

What on earth is he talking about, I thought. This box was a tiny little thing. *Could it be the keys?* I had no idea what he was talking about, and I was as confused as ever. But I quickly realized that I wasn't going to get any more information out of him, so I just opened the box.

It was a stunning gold necklace.

I was amazed and dumbfounded.

Well, it's beautiful, but it's not resembling anything close to a motorcycle, I thought. I much preferred the necklace, but I wanted to know what he was getting at. I admired the wonderful jewelry in front of me as I tried to make sense of the situation.

"James, this is so beautiful, but I still don't know what you mean. How is this your motorcycle?"

"While you were gone," he began, "I did some thinking about us. I knew that something was off. I realized how unhappy you were during the last ride we took together, and I wanted to show you how much you mean to me. So, I sold my motorcycle and used the money to buy you that necklace."

Right then and there, I knew that he was the guy for me.

I couldn't believe a guy would do something like that for me. I knew that his motorcycle meant so much to him, but the fact that he didn't hesitate to make it secondary to our relationship instantly told me that he was in this for real. And I knew that I felt the same way.

We made the relationship official, and after dating for a time, we got engaged.

Dad was so excited. He was so happy to see I had found so much joy with a stand-up man who loved me. I could imagine it isn't easy for a father to find out that his daughter is dating someone, but Dad was always so kind to James. It meant a lot to Dad to see that James continually demonstrated his loyalty to me in so many wonderful ways. Dad gave us his full blessing, and we were so excited.

My mom didn't have quite the same enthusiasm, but I do have to acknowledge the positive role that both of my parents played for the occasion. They generously agreed to pay for the day so that James and I wouldn't have to blow our scant young adult budget, which was an incredible gesture. Finances are a tricky subject to talk about in a family, but I was amazed at my parents' decision to pay for our entire wedding. No amount of gratitude felt like enough to show just how thankful I was for that.

Although they were willing to sign the check, my mother didn't want to be involved with any of the planning. It was quite the contrast compared to what most mothers like to do, especially the ones paying for the event; usually, they feel entitled to have a lot of say over how things are done. But not my mom. I think she just wanted to give me the money and let me take care of everything myself so she wouldn't have to deal with me. She never seemed to be happy for me when something good was happening in my life. If anything, it seemed to annoy her.

It was a strange feeling as a daughter to feel like her mother was totally disengaged from the whole wedding planning process. On the plus side, I didn't have to deal with one of those nightmarish situations like those reality wedding shows (however "real" those might be) since my mother didn't care to be a part of any of it. But I'd be lying if I said I was totally fine with the arrangement. As damaged as our history had been, she was still my mother, and this was my official send-off into a new life. It was a bit sad not to have her around during that process, especially since I didn't have any sisters.

Even still, we didn't let that situation spoil the joy of our wedding. It was an amazing day that went by in the blink of an eye, just like much of the 27 years did after high school. We got married and saw a number of our friends get married. We worked, went to night school, changed jobs, and moved around a lot. Friends came and went. We went through the rhythms of life. James and I went through a number of transitions during that time, which I'll do my best to recount over the next few chapters.

It really does go by so fast. It almost feels like yesterday that I was a young woman sitting in James's passenger seat. Maybe I'm just feeling extra nostalgic as I write down all these memories, but they've made me the person I am today. I could never have anticipated that my life would go in the direction it did, but there were so many fantastic people who made it special. It's important to hold onto those people.

James has certainly been one of those people for me. Once we got together and officially started our family, he went many years without another motorcycle. Even though he would have loved to have one, he put the needs of our household first because that's the kind of man he is. Much later, once our children were grown and out of the house, he ended up getting another motorcycle for himself and has loved it ever since. I thought it was well-deserved.

I often hear single people wondering how they know when they've found "the one," and I wondered this myself as a single person as well. While I don't think there's a one-size-fits-all answer to that question, I think a key factor for James and me was how easy it was for the two of us to be together. In the early days, I still had those early relationship jitters, but I still wanted to be around him. That's partially why it was so hard to step back in our relationship for a while because I missed spending time with him. I felt like I could be doing any activity under the sun and still want him to be around. When we finally got together and started our family, it just felt like the natural progression of where our relationship was meant to go. It was a truly beautiful thing to share that with James.

Chapter 10:

Building Family Memories

The lives of young families move so quickly.

That can be interpreted in a few different ways. On the one hand, there's the physical pace of the day, which can feel quite hectic at times, but it's only after the fact that we fully realize everything that has happened. For instance, James and I moved to three different states while our kids were growing up. It was a lot of organizing and physical labor without ever seemingly having enough time in the day to do everything. Moving is always exhausting at the time, but once I saw my whole life packed into a truck, I forgot about all of the aches and pains. There was nothing that could've quite prepared me for that feeling. Suddenly, I forgot about all the heavy lifting and just stared in awe at how quickly everything seemed to have gone.

And then, there are the big milestones we reached as a family to further emphasize how fast everything goes by. Between volunteering at our children's schools, attending their piano lessons and recitals, and watching sports events together, it's unbelievable to think about how quickly they grow up. I remember little memories here and there, like my son attending yearly Boy Scout camping trips with my husband. My dad would tag along for the weekend as well, assuming the role of "cook" for the troop. But it all is a blur after a while, even though the memories themselves are still so distinct. It's hard to explain, but at the end of the day, I just have to step back and admire the life my husband and I have built together. I wouldn't trade back a single move or memory that we formed, even if it was a bit chaotic while it was happening.

Because we experienced so many changes as a young family, I've decided to refer to this section of the book in terms of a 27-year time gap instead of our locations. It would be far too complicated to keep track of the places we visited between our houses and vacations since we got around to many different places.

Although we never had a summer home like I had in Auburn, I'm glad our travels exposed my kids to new people and locations. I'm grateful they had the chance to see so many new things. There was no joy quite like watching one of my children see something new and exciting for the first time. It felt like I was re-experiencing it for the first time, too. It still melts my heart to think about those moments and how precious children are.

As for the adults, our transition years didn't quite have the same wonder and amazement all the time. During one of our moves, James and I were having a new house built for us, which was already a massive undertaking. One day, my parents came up to visit the house and see how the progress was progressing. At one point, when we were all in a similar area, my dad brushed up against my shoulder and whispered something close to my ear.

"Sweetie, could we talk for a second?"

I was surprised by the question. My dad wasn't a gossipy or secretive person, so pulling me aside to talk seemed out of character for him. Even still, I wanted to know what was going on.

"Yeah, for sure, Dad."

He walked with me to a different part of the house so that we were out of earshot of my mother. His eyebrows were bunched together, and his eyes looked distraught. I was almost getting worried for his well-being, but he had other news.

"Okay, so when your mother and I found out that you were moving into a new home, I wanted to buy you guys something as a housewarming present. After a bit of brainstorming, I thought a new dishwasher might be helpful, so I wanted to go pick one of those out for you. But…"

He couldn't make eye contact with me as he spoke, so I wanted to encourage him to keep going.

"What is it, Dad?"

"But when I ran the idea by your mother, she didn't seem as keen. She kept on saying how it was impractical and that we shouldn't be making such a big purchase for you guys. I tried to talk her into it, but she wouldn't budge. I'm so sorry, honey. I didn't want to show up here empty-handed, and I've been feeling terrible about it all day."

He had no reason to feel terrible. *He* was the one who wanted to do something so sweet for James and me and our kids. It was my mother who should've felt terrible about her actions, but she showed no hint of remorse for the entire day.

The thing is, I didn't even care about the dishwasher specifically; James and I were already planning on buying one when we moved in, so we hadn't lost anything. The thought of my mother purposefully turning down Dad's request to do something nice for us made my blood boil. She had all the power in the situation and unilaterally decided that it wasn't something she felt was worthwhile. Again, I wasn't expecting them to do anything for us, and we were in a financial position where we could take care of everything ourselves. But if they had chosen to do something that would've helped James and me out, we would've warmly received that. Unfortunately, that wasn't something that my mother felt was important enough to do.

I still remember how sad my father looked during that conversation, almost like a puppy dog that knew it had done something wrong. But my dad only wanted to do something nice, and there was nothing wrong with that.

Years later, James and I moved into another house, and I went shopping for window treatments with my mom. It was a good excuse for an outing, and sometimes it can be helpful to have a second opinion on household items. But before and during our shopping trip, I made it a point to let her know about our budget.

"Mom, we have to stay within this amount," I'd tell her. "James and I can't afford to spend any more than this right now. We can look at different brands and whatnot, but we have to spend less than this."

"Don't talk to me like I'm a child, Emma. I know what a budget is."

Not a great start, but I made sure I repeated myself many times. It didn't matter. Every time I picked out some blinds or drapes, I was met with a similar type of response.

"Mom, what do you think of this one?" I asked.

"I don't like that."

"Okay, well, what about this?"

"No."

"This one's kinda neat."

"Really? *That?*"

"I thought it was nice."

"You have no taste. None of your choices are good."

And what was her response to that? To continuously choose a more expensive style that was outside of our budget. She may have known what a budget was, but sticking to a budget, though... that was something I don't think she understood.

"Mom, I told you we can't afford that," I'd say.

"This is the best one," she'd say. "Just take it, and I'll pay for it."

Wow. This was a surprising gesture of compassion coming from my mom. "You don't need to do that," I said. "We're fine to just get the cheaper ones."

She didn't respond to my comment but just called the salesman over. "Excuse me... Hi, my daughter would like to pay for these."

"That sounds good," he said. "She only needs to pay the deposit now, and then she can cover the remaining once they come in."

I was shocked. Perhaps this was my mother's way of making amends after refusing to pay for the dishwasher. I'd never spoken to her about that, but I wondered if she had some lingering guilt that prompted her to pay for these treatments.

I paid the deposit at the front of the store. "Thank you, Mom. I really appreciate this."

She said nothing and kept looking straight ahead. After we finished up, we left the store.

A few weeks later, I got a call to say that the window treatments were ready to be picked up. I called my mother to give her the news.

"Hi Mom," I said. "The window treatments are ready now."

"Wow, that was quick," she said.

I waited for a second to see if there was any follow-up to that remark. Nothing. I didn't want to push too hard for the money right away, so I let it go, and we carried on talking about something else.

I didn't say anything about the treatments for about a week, but she still hadn't mentioned them. I decided to bring it up again in conversation.

"Hey, Mom, the window treatments that I ordered came in last week."

"You already told me that."

Based on the way she barked back at me, I was intimidated to bring it up again. I got the impression that she wasn't going to pay for anything. She'd tricked me into spending more money than I needed to spend. It felt like sabotage; it felt as if she wanted to have her choice be the one we went with at the expense of my financial comfort.

I didn't bother asking her for the money. I went to the store by myself and picked up the treatments.

We didn't speak about it for the longest time. Eventually, years after the event had taken place, I thought I'd mention it again—not out of malice or anything, but in more of a friendly, hey-remember-this kind of way.

"I remember when you talked me into getting the more expensive window treatments," I said. "You'd promised to pay for them in the store, but I felt weird asking about it once they came in. Just wondering, were you ever planning on paying me back for those?"

"What do you want me to do; pay for them now?"

"Well, no, of course not. I was just wondering."

And that was the end of that.

That incident was particularly hurtful because it felt like my mother was actively rooting against me. Like I said earlier, the dishwasher incident definitely stung, but it didn't cause my situation to change at all. The window treatments also didn't ruin my bank account or anything, but they did cause James and me to spend more money than we'd been intending. I'd made my budget explicitly clear to my mother, and she repeatedly went over it and manipulated me into buying something that I wasn't comfortable paying for on my own. I think she wanted to show that she had "bested" me in some way—like she wanted me to get the drapes that she wanted regardless of how I felt about it. Well, congratulations to her. She won that round.

I know I've mentioned a few negative memories of my mother in this chapter, but all in all, she was actually easier to get along with when the kids were young (I know—it shocked me, too). She loved being around babies and actually helped out a lot with babysitting when the kids were young. That said, it was my dad's idea; he told my mom to quit her job to babysit my children because he didn't want his grandchildren going to daycare, and she agreed to do it. Being a grandmother made her happy in a way I'd never seen before. It made me wonder if she had ever been that happy with me at one point, which made me further question what had gone wrong between us. But even still, it was really nice for me to see that she had a softer side to her that came out when we had the kids.

Every so often, though, she still regressed to her old self.

As I watched my kids grow up, I became nostalgic for my own childhood memories. I knew that my parents had some footage of me when I was young (for those who know what "Super 8" film is, that's the stuff we had), but I hadn't seen it in years. I thought it would be nice to revisit my early years, not just for myself but for my children to see as well. I thought they'd get a good kick out of seeing what their grandparents and I were like when I was young.

So, one day, I decided to ask my mom about it.

"Hey Mom, do you remember how Dad took all those videos of me when I was a kid? Do you know where that stuff is? I'd like to take a look at it and show the kids."

She almost looked annoyed by the question, as if it was a stupid thing to be asking. "I threw all that stuff out years ago. It was just clutter. Took up too much space. We didn't need it anymore. You're grown up, after all."

Well, *I* certainly would've made use of it!

"Wait, so you don't have any other video footage of me?"

"Videos, pictures… Yeah, I got rid of all that stuff."

"School projects?"

"Why would you need to keep any of that junk? It was just a few pieces of messy handwriting and poorly-glued construction paper. We needed the space, and they didn't serve any purpose."

"But that was my childhood! That was all the evidence I had of most of my memories as a kid. And you don't have any of it?"

"Well, what do you want me to say?"

I'm sorry would've been a good start, but that certainly wasn't going to happen. It was almost like she just wanted to erase me.

So, I don't have any memorabilia from my childhood. All of the stories I'm sharing with you are coming purely from my memory because I don't have any physical items that capture them. My mother threw out any trace of my younger years because she felt they had no utility.

If there was any silver lining to losing my childhood belongings, it motivated me to do the exact opposite for my own children. I've saved nearly everything for them from the time they were babies. It's probably too much, in all honesty. But I remember how much it hurt to discover that there was no evidence of my childhood, and I never wanted my own kids to go through that. Plus, their memories meant a lot to me, too. I wanted them to have full access to as much of their younger years as possible. I figured they could decide what they wanted to keep and leave behind once they'd grown up and moved out. They've since gone through that process, and I hold onto the things they've left behind.

I also made an effort to pass on the traditions that stuck out to me from my childhood as a way to pass on that legacy. For instance, when my kids were young, I made them omelets with grape jelly, just like the ones that Grandma Joan would make for me. It felt like a fitting way to honor a wonderful woman, make delicious food for my kids, and cling to the memories I still have from my youth. It felt like I was passing a torch in carrying on old traditions while creating new memories with my own family, which brought me so much joy to see.

Of course, it still hurt to know that I could never see my younger self again. After 54 years, though, I think I've discovered that there was a bigger reason for that than just taking up space.

It took me until my adulthood to realize that my mother was a narcissist.

Chapter 11:

Mother Doesn't Know Best

It all made so much sense.

Ditching my childhood memories. Manipulating people into getting her way. Refusing to admit when she was wrong. Getting annoyed at anything that inconvenienced her. Lacking compassion for others who are in pain. Always needing to come out on top, even when no one wanted there to be a competition.

There was a way to explain all of it. My mother was a narcissist.

But before I get too far ahead of myself, I want to define what I mean when I say "narcissism" or "narcissist" because I know that could be interpreted in many different ways. After years of research and lived experience, here's how I understand the concepts.

Narcissism is a disorder in which a person has an inflated sense of self-importance; therefore, a narcissist is someone who is diagnosed with that condition. A narcissist's egotistical thought patterns become so harmful to the point where they need constant praise and validation from other people to maintain their vanity. At the same time, the narcissist will exploit those same people without guilt because they cannot extend empathy or sympathy for anyone other than themselves.

A narcissist's desire to have their way trumps everything else, so they have little regard for the repercussions of their actions on other people. As long as the narcissist's wants and needs are satisfied, the end justifies the means of getting there. In addition, if something goes wrong, narcissists refuse to assume any blame or responsibility for it. Instead, they will project that wrongdoing onto someone else, often to an exaggerated degree. However, they feel justified in their behavior because it allows them to always get their way; in their mind, their way is the best way.

All of this rang so true when I heard it for the first time. It made so much sense to put a name to everything that it almost scared me how accurate it was in places. It felt like someone had gone into my brain and pulled out all of these suspicions I'd had of my mother but I was too afraid to say them out loud. I can't express just how reassuring it was to hear that this was not only a thing but a serious thing that could be diagnosed. No wonder I felt so stressed out around my mother all the time!

But the real kicker for me was recognizing that this was an *abnormal* trait. Before coming to this realization, I just thought that this was the way of life for everyone. Everybody has their quirks, and I'd figured, "Well, that's Mom's quirk, I guess. She's demanding and uncompromising without seeming to care about anyone else's needs if they disrupt hers." I'd excused her behaviors for a long time until I realized these weren't normal. She knew what she was doing in taking advantage of people, and I didn't have to try to dig her out of a hole that she'd made for herself.

After years of feeling like I'd been trying to understand my mother, this discovery was one of the first times where I felt understood as the person on the receiving end of it. Throughout the years, I remember it being so hard to explain my mother's behavior to people who'd see glimpses of her narcissism. I'd try to make light of it and just say, "Oh, she's just like that. It's no big deal," but deep down, I knew it was a huge deal. I was just afraid that no one else would believe me because my mother was exceptional at spinning a story in her favor.

Some of her family members told me later in life that she was also a habitual liar, which was a huge breakthrough for me to realize as well. Apparently, she had been telling lies since childhood. It wasn't just me whom she was upset with all the time, although I received the brunt of it once I came into the picture. I didn't know why she was the way she was, but I guess she had been this way for as long as people can remember.

And some of you reading this might wonder, *Well, gee, how could you ever fall for someone like that?* But I've seen the way she acts around people and she can be very charming. Narcissists know how to make themselves look good in just about any situation. The confidence with which they speak causes you to second-guess yourself because they sound like they know what they're talking about. Only after you remove yourself from the situation and think about it more rationally, though, can you start to decipher the truth from the lies. But if you have emotional ties to a narcissist, it only makes it more difficult to separate those two things. And by the time you realize it, it's often too late.

Once she married my father, she thought she had his love and affection for life. But when I came around, there was suddenly another female in his life whom he loved with all his heart. I wouldn't be surprised if my mother felt threatened by me at a young age because I took some of the attention off of her. Children are a lot of work and require an immense amount of time, and I think my mother felt like she had to compete with me for my father's attention. And as far as it was within her power, she was determined to win. But she would never let people on the outside know how she acted at home or how she treated me, so I felt like I was trapped.

Part of the reason for my complicated relationship with my mother was that I'd be inextricably tied to her as her daughter. I didn't want to be fake with her, but sometimes it was difficult to have any kind of positive emotion with her when I knew she wouldn't make any effort to show that to me. Birthdays and Mother's Day would make the situation even weirder because I'd feel obligated to do something for her while wrestling with my own feelings.

I always catered to my mother on Mother's Day. Other than her birthday, it was the one day in the year when I felt like she truly deserved to be pampered for a day. But since I was the one who'd made her a mother, I felt like the onus of Mother's Day was really on me to make sure she was happy. So, I wouldn't hold back. I'd give her gifts and either make her dinner or take her out for dinner. I tried to treat her for the day, and she absolutely loved being doted on.

She never reciprocated after I became a mother. Over the last few decades, I never once received a card, gift, or even a happy Mother's Day wish from her. I guess the day was only ever allowed to be about her, and recognizing me as a mother would've taken some of the spotlight off of her. But it still hurt me to think that there wasn't so much as a phone call from her to spend 30 seconds wishing me a good day.

After many years, I decided to address it with her.

"Mom, can I ask you something?"

"Yeah, what?"

"Over the years, I noticed that you'd never sent anything to me for Mother's Day. I don't mean to be needy, but I *am* also a mother, after all. I know how much that day means to you, but did it ever occur to you to think of sending something to me for Mother's Day?"

"What for? You're not my mother."

Apparently, being the mother of her grandchildren wasn't enough of a reason for her to give me a call and say, "Happy Mother's Day, Emma."

I shouldn't have expected anything from her, but I wanted to hold onto a little bit of hope that bringing this to her attention would spark something in her. One of the reasons I find narcissism difficult to talk about is that I don't want to sound like I'm boxing people into stereotypes or speaking in generic, extreme terms. Of course, people can grow and change, which is why I don't want to be too judgmental. But I think it's also important to recognize when people are unwilling to change, no matter how many chances we give them.

I kept trying to give my mother opportunities to apologize for things she'd done. I didn't want her to feel like I was picking on her for mistakes she'd made, but I also wanted her to be held accountable and know that I hadn't forgotten how she hurt me. I would've been much more willing to forgive her if she'd genuinely apologized and made an effort to try and change her ways. But my mother, like a lot of narcissists, seemed incapable of change, which is what made the next big event in our family's life so difficult.

After 45 years of marriage, my mother decided she wanted a divorce.

It sent shockwaves throughout my family and our social circles. If anyone would've wanted and been justified in getting a divorce, it should've been my dad. He had every reason to want to remove himself from my mother, and I'm not even sure that he knew everything that was going on in her personal life. But in spite of all that, he upheld his vows and maintained his loyalty to my mom while she was unfaithful and ungrateful toward him.

When asked the reason for wanting a divorce, my mother's response was, "I don't like the way he talks to me."

Really? After 45 years, you're just now realizing that you don't like the way he talks to you?

I find it hard to believe this was some massive barrier to their relationship that they couldn't get past. First of all, communication patterns don't suddenly take a nosedive after being married for that long. Spouses know each other inside and out by that point, and they get much better at reading each other and understanding each other as time goes on. And secondly, Dad wasn't the kind of person to speak negatively of people. As I said above, when my mother was at her worst, he still wanted to honor her in the way he spoke about her. In the middle of the divorce proceedings themselves, he never once said a nasty word against her. Even when it was just the two of them behind closed doors, I don't believe my father's speech toward my mother was nearly as bad as she said it was.

Personally, I think she was just looking for attention. In classic narcissistic fashion, she wanted to be at the center of everyone's conversations by portraying herself as this oppressed victim of an unhappy marriage. In reality, though, she had it far better with my dad than she would've had it if she'd married any other guy. She couldn't have gotten a better marriage with anyone else. No man would have simultaneously provided for her and taken as much of her crap as my father did. But apparently, that wasn't enough for her to want to stay with him. Nothing is ever enough for her.

My parents went through all of the divorce proceedings and negotiations. They split up all of our possessions and sold off things that they weren't going to use anymore, including our beloved summer home at the shore. Everybody adored that house and thought we'd have it in our family forever. It was a sad day to turn in those keys for good and drive away thinking that everything would be different from here on out.

It was so embarrassing to explain it to people I knew. They almost always expressed genuine concern for the situation, which was very sweet, but I wasn't sure how to respond. I knew how selfish my mother's motivations were behind the scenes, which made it difficult to make excuses for her. I'd been doing it all my life, but now that I was old enough to realize what she was doing, I felt this pit of disgust in my stomach any time I tried to stick up for her. It was a one-sided divorce that she instigated, yet I still felt that I had to make her look decent. I wrestled with that constantly.

Parent-child relationships can get increasingly more complicated as the child becomes an adult. On the one hand, the child becomes self-assured as a functioning adult who's capable of developing their own thoughts and feelings about their parents' methods. But on the other hand, they're still their parents' child. And their parents will always see them as their child. It didn't matter how much I grew up; my mother would always see me as this annoying nuisance of a kid who took some of Dad's attention away from her. It was frustrating, to say the least, because I never felt like she would see me as an adult in my own right.

The flip side to that scenario is that, as the child grows into an adult, they also realize that their parents are just people, too. They're just trying their best to make their way through this world without really being sure of what to do a lot of the time. A part of me wanted my parents to fight for their marriage, but I also wanted my dad to be free. I had to learn to let them make their own decisions regardless of the opinion I'd come to form about the situation. If divorce was what my mother felt was best, I could make my views known, but I couldn't stop her from going through with that.

As it turned out, divorce wasn't what my mother wanted after all.

About a month after the divorce had been finalized, my parents were suddenly back together. It was just as shocking to hear that news as it was to hear that they were getting divorced in the first place. What was the purpose of any of that? All that hassle and stress, just to undo it after a month? And after all of the financial pressure that came from the proceedings, it seemed like an even bigger burden to go back to the way things were.

Well, I knew who the culprit was. Once the lawyers were dismissed and she was alone in her house, I think my mother missed having someone to take care of her. There was no one around to admire her and do things for her anymore. As soon as she realized how much she missed the attention, she somehow convinced my dad to give it another shot.

I had no idea that my mother was capable of stooping to these kinds of lows. All I knew was that I was in for another embarrassing tour of explanations to try to give to everyone. Understandably, they had a lot of questions that I felt I shouldn't have had to answer.

It was a miserable time for everyone, but it paled in comparison to what the year 2008 had in store. That would become one of the worst years of my life.

Chapter 12:

2008

Leading up to 2008, my family and I were navigating some major changes.

One of the most significant changes during that time involved James' job requiring us to move to Wyoming. Now, when I say that I didn't want to go at all, that's me making a major understatement. I vehemently opposed it. I was so tired of having to pick up my life and move somewhere new after just starting to feel settled into a new place. I had already moved around a fair bit between my childhood and my adult years and just wanted to settle down somewhere close to family. A move to Wyoming would mean moving several time zones over to the West, where neither one of us had ever lived before. In other words, it was the complete opposite of what I wanted.

Because I love my husband, I eventually agreed to go, but not without kicking and screaming. Wyoming was so far removed from everything I'd ever known, and because I'd never made such a big move before, I was scared. I didn't know what a major move would mean for our relationships with our family and friends, and I felt terrible for my children, too, since they had to start at a new school. But I'm thankful to report that everything turned out okay.

Wyoming was a lovely place for James and me to live and raise our family. We met so many wonderful people there, and our family still goes back to visit every once in a while. If nothing had changed and we would've ended up staying there longer, I would've been okay with that. However, when we realized that we could move back to Connecticut in August of 2008, we took the opportunity to move back home. I'd actually adjusted so well to life in Wyoming that I was initially reluctant to go back to Connecticut. But it was perfect timing for our family since our kids could get settled back into Connecticut before the start of the new school year.

Shortly before our move back, Dad also retired in July of 2008 at age 65. It was a well-deserved retirement. He'd spent over 40 years working hard and supporting his family, which wasn't always an easy thing to do. But he never complained about it, simply putting his head down and doing the task at hand.

Dad never had the kind of job where he had to bring his work home with him, and I came to realize how much of a blessing that was later on in life. Don't get me wrong; I have nothing against people who want to climb the professional ladder. I think it's great that they want to make the most of their skills and see how high they can soar. But my dad was someone who wanted to separate his work time from his home time, and working on the dump truck allowed him to do that. Once the end of his workday rolled around, he could sign out and come home ready to fully devote himself to his family.

I think that was a major contributing factor behind my dad and I sharing such a close relationship. Because he worked the job he did, he was able to spend uninterrupted time with me and watch me grow up. That said, he must've had to work extra hard during those work hours to make sure that he'd be emotionally available for me and my mom when he came home. So, when his retirement came around, and he could fully embrace his new phase of life, I thought it was more than well-deserved.

Unfortunately, that embrace didn't last for very long.

Also in August of 2008, only one month after beginning his retirement, my dad was diagnosed with renal cell carcinoma. And it was terminal.

I'd never heard of a "renal cell carcinoma" before that diagnosis. I did a Google search and learned that it's a scientific term for a type of kidney cancer. I also found out the likely cause was related to the 9/11 cleanup initiative my dad had taken part in. Being exposed to all those fumes for a while was almost certainly the reason for his cancer diagnosis.

During my research, I also discovered that there was a nationwide $7 billion trust fund available for workers who had been involved in the cleanup. I began looking into this more to see if there was anything that could be done to compensate for what had happened to my father. Almost immediately, I started getting emails from lawyers. I told my mom about it, but she wasn't interested. Not exactly shocking to me. I decided to look into it further anyways, responding to one of the lawyers who'd reached out to me. We had some correspondence back and forth, and I eventually made an appointment for him to meet my parents at their house.

I had no idea that any of this stuff existed, and I was thankful that someone was willing to help explain it all to me. From that point onward, I made all the appointments with lawyers, filled out all the paperwork, and drove both of my parents to all the meetings. Oh yeah—once my mother learned that there could potentially be money involved, she suddenly took a keen interest in how everything would play out. Interesting.

Dad's health kept declining, and it was getting harder and harder for him to attend those depositions. It was hard for me to watch his body break down, but I wanted to make sure justice was served in some capacity. At one particular meeting, he made it a point to state why he agreed to go through these proceedings.

"I don't want this to be very complicated," he said, struggling to muster enough energy to speak each word. "The only reason why I'm agreeing to go through with this is for my wife and my daughter. I want Doris to have a comfortable life without having to worry about anything related to money. And I want Emma's mortgage to be fully paid off with the money so that she and James and the kids can have a long and happy life together."

The lawyer sat right in front of him, hearing every word he spoke just as my mom and I had heard it. I'll get back to this later.

It was bad enough to have to go through more legal procedures after my parents' divorce, but doing so while my dad was enduring a horrible illness made it far worse. He required constant care to make sure that he was doing okay, from walking down the hallway to eating his meals. It was so hard to see him in that condition because I knew he never wanted anyone to make a big fuss about him. It really bothered him when he couldn't drive anymore because he had always been the driver both at work and at home. After being the provider for so many years, he was now the one who needed to be provided for. I think he always struggled with that feeling, regardless of how many times I'd tell him that he wasn't a burden to us. Cancer is a horrible disease.

Hospice workers would come to my parents' house for an hour or two each day to look after him and see how he was doing. One day, the nurse was over while I was making dinner for my parents at their place. After placing our meal in the oven, I had a few minutes to spare. I figured that since the nurse was around, it would give me a breather to clean out my purse. I'd been meaning to do it for a while and desperately needed to reorganize everything but I just couldn't find a free moment to do it until now. So, I sat at the kitchen table and proceeded to take things out of my purse.

Of course, this was the exact moment when my mother walked into the room.

"What the hell are you doing?" she practically screamed at me. "You don't have anything better to do at a time like this?"

"What? No! I just—"

"All you can think about is cleaning your purse while your father is fighting for his life. I didn't think you could be so selfish. Pathetic."

I was just waiting for dinner to cook! Plus, the nurse was with Dad. I was fully prepared to take over for her once she left. Everything was fine. I don't know what my mother's problem was, but she definitely had a problem. She proceeded to barge into Dad's room while the nurse was still in there, all aggravated over a non-issue.

"I don't even know why my daughter comes here. She's useless to me."

I could overhear her telling the nurse her version of the story as I just sat there crying. Could I ever do anything to please her?

Despite my best attempts, my mother kept trying to make me look like the bad guy. She would take one little moment out of context and blow it up into some huge story to make it seem like a big deal when it really wasn't. In this case, I would've just been in the nurse's way if I'd gone to see him at that moment. Plus, I was making the dinner that *she* would be eating. But I never got any acknowledgment for that.

I asked my mom several times to stay with us. We had better hospitals in our town, not to mention the support of James and me to take care of some of the day-to-day living responsibilities. We lived 120 miles away from my parents, which meant that I'd have to either use vacation time or work remotely on days when I went to see them. It would've made everything easier for everyone if they had stayed with us, but she always declined. She used different excuses about not wanting to put Dad through more difficulties, but I think she just never wanted to stay with me any longer than she had to. I pushed back a little bit at first but quickly realized that it wasn't worth the effort. If I wanted to go see Dad, I just made the trip myself. I would go as often as I could, usually staying for a few days at a time, but it was hard to get away. I couldn't leave my children, husband, or job for too long, but I wanted to make an effort.

I would go to their place for two reasons: one, to spend time with my dad, and two, to give my mom a break and get out of the house. Personal issues aside, it was a lot of work for my mom to take care of Dad, and I could recognize that. When I came over, I was happy to take over the grocery shopping, cooking, and dish-cleaning responsibilities for a time, in addition to tending to my dad. Whatever would help my Dad get the care he needs while giving my mother a chance to get out for a while was what I was willing to do.

What I didn't care for was the fact that my mother would walk in circles around the house, acting like she was so busy when I was over. If she wanted a break, she could've just said so and taken a full break. I would've understood that. But instead, it had to be this whole song and dance to try to appear like she was working too hard to see what I was doing. That part of it annoyed me, but it was almost to be expected at this point.

But I never wanted to let my grievances with my mother affect the kind of care my father received. At first, it was difficult to see his body slowly wear down, but when his cancer spread to his brain, it became so much worse. It got to a point where he didn't know who I was anymore. It's one of the most difficult experiences in life to watch someone you love grow progressively sicker. Although we could try to slow down the process, we were also bracing ourselves for what would come next.

Like I said earlier, I didn't want to move back from Wyoming at first, but now, I'm glad we did. I wouldn't have wanted to be anywhere else during such a trying time for him because I knew he would've done the same for us. When we did live in Wyoming, my children called him to ask if he could come to watch them in a school play the following week. He replied immediately, saying, "I'll be there." Sure enough, he drove 30 hours from Connecticut to Wyoming to watch an hour-long play because that's the kind of man he was. Naturally, when he started going through this health crisis, I couldn't imagine any other outcome other than spending as much time with him as I could.

Everyone in the family made sure that they could be together on Christmas. I remember feeding him turkey and sweet potato baby food because he couldn't swallow food anymore. James had taken a week off of work to take care of him right around Christmas. He changed him, bathed him, and fed him, almost as if to complete the cycle of life and care for the elderly as one would with a baby.

James left to come home on the Saturday after Christmas. Dad died on that Sunday.

Just four months after being diagnosed and five months after retiring, my father was gone. I was glad that he didn't have to suffer anymore, but it just didn't seem fair that, after working so hard for so many years, a wonderful man like him never got to enjoy his retirement.

I think I felt worse for my children than I did for myself. Of course, I was devastated, but I also had five decades of wonderful, loving memories with him. My children, however, were just getting to know him, and they'd be missing out on having such a great person in their lives.

He was the best grandfather ever. When I announced that I was pregnant, my dad went out and bought a carriage the very next day in preparation for his first grandchild. He couldn't do enough for his grandchildren, just like he had done for me. He loved taking them for long walks in the carriage and going with them to McDonald's. One of my children's favorite memories is of my dad making them ice cream sodas with grape soda and mint ice cream. It was a combination that most people would cringe over, but my kids loved it. Many years later, they had a blast recreating those sodas in memory of him.

How many people can you honestly say have never let you down? And I mean never, not once? My father is that person for me. I could depend on him any day, at any time, and for any reason. He never refused and always helped me with a smile.

A piece of my heart was gone forever.

My mother's brother sent me a sympathy card shortly after Dad's death. He wrote in it, "Too bad the good one in that marriage had to go first."

Chapter 13:

The Aftermath

I wanted my father's ashes in my home.

My mother knew this. She'd always seen how close my dad and I had been over the years, so I don't think it came as any surprise to her to learn that I wanted to keep his ashes. She told me she didn't want them at her house. Fair enough. So, I picked up the ashes from the funeral home and kept them at my house.

Meanwhile, James had designed a beautiful ceramic urn to hold Dad's ashes. My husband does pottery as a hobby, and he's incredibly skilled at it. He has made some stunning pieces over the years that have filled our home with wonderful, one-of-a-kind items of all sorts. There's nothing quite like the unique touch of a homemade object that can stay in a family for generations. And for someone as special as my dad, I felt like he deserved an original urn of some kind to preserve his memory.

I figured that I should mention this to my mother.

"Mom, James just finished the urn for Dad's ashes," I told her. "You should really see it. It's stunning. He's outdone himself with this one."

"That's nice. Now we can go drop it off at the cemetery," she said.

"Drop it off? What do you mean?" I asked.

"Oh, I went to the cemetery last week and bought a crypt for his ashes. Once you'd finished making whatever container you wanted for them, I figured we could go together to bury it in there."

Excuse me?

"Umm… What? You didn't think of talking to me about that first?!"

"You wouldn't want some old ashes in your home, Emma. They just sit there and collect dust. There's no purpose in keeping them."

"It's not just about utility, Mom. And they're not just 'some old ashes,' they're *Dad's* ashes! That was all we had left of him, and you thought it would be better to lock him away in some vault?!"

"Don't yell at me. I did this for your own good. You'd just look at them and turn into a blubbering mess. They were just gonna get in the way, so I took care of everything."

"But I wanted them! I specifically told you that I wanted them! James did all of that hard work, and nobody will be able to see it. And you didn't even bother to say anything!"

"This isn't a debate, Emma. It's done. We're going."

Unbelievable.

My mother had stooped to some pretty low lows in the past, but this was a new level that absolutely infuriated me. But what set me off was how she tried to frame the situation as though she was doing me and my family a favor. She made it sound like she was trying to protect us from all of the heartaches we'd experienced from looking at his ashes, which apparently served no real purpose. But she blatantly went against my wishes and ensured that I wouldn't be able to have my way. The fact that it was at my father's expense just felt like she was rubbing salt in the wound.

It was so hard to go to the cemetery and watch him being put in a crypt. As I stood there, I kept thinking about what would happen when my mom passed. Since I was the executor of her will, I could get my dad's ashes back at that time, although I wasn't sure when that time would come. Until then, I had to leave him behind. It was one of the most difficult things I've ever had to do.

When my mother would do something like this, I knew I could turn to my dad for comfort. He wouldn't explicitly take a side since he had loyalty to both my mother and me, but he would do everything in his power to make sure that I knew I was loved. And I did. I knew he loved me, at least. Once he died, though, this situation just felt like a horrible preview of what the rest of my life would look like with only her in the picture. And, to an extent, it kind of was.

Case in point, I broke the tibia bone in my lower leg long after everything with my dad had happened. It was a bad break, to the point where I needed surgery and couldn't bear weight on it for eight weeks afterward. That would be hard enough for anyone to do when they just have to look after themselves, never mind someone with dependents. To my surprise, my mother volunteered to stay with me and help out around the house. The gesture definitely took me aback, and I had my hesitations about living with her for two months, but I thought it was gracious of her to offer, so I took her up on it.

In hindsight, it would've been more accurate to say that she came to our house with the intent of being a martyr rather than a mother. Yes, she stayed with us for several weeks as I recovered from a pretty significant surgery, but she was hardly helpful. Every morning, I would haul myself out of bed and into a wheelchair, which I'd wheel into the kitchen. I'd start preparing breakfasts for my children along with coffee for my mother, which I don't drink. All the while, she slept. Once the kids were gone, my mother would put the laundry in the washer and dryer. I would then fold everything at the kitchen table and prepare nightly dinners (whatever could be done from sitting at the table, at least).

The most challenging chore was definitely vacuuming. I remember having to carry the vacuum on my lap as I shuffled myself onto the steps and bum-scooched my way down the stairs. I'd proceed to vacuum the floor while using a walker. I don't know what my mother was doing that whole time, but not once did she offer to vacuum the floors or do anything beyond the bare minimum. Rather, she told me it would be a good exercise for me. How thoughtful.

But on top of doing little to no work, she was in a bad mood the whole time she was with us. Our bathroom was on the second floor of our house, but there was no way that I could get up the steps to do that, so I had a commode set up on the first floor. The tasks that my mom did help out with were driving me to doctor's appointments and emptying my commode each day (personally, if I was dead-set on only doing a few tasks, I wouldn't have picked emptying a commode, but to each their own). Our family kept using the bathroom as per usual while I stayed on the first floor as much as possible.

After eight weeks had passed, I was finally able to make my way up the stairs to the full bathroom. When I saw what was inside, I was shocked at the condition it was in. It was horrendous. The mess was so atrocious that I couldn't even begin to describe it. It would be one thing if my mother was working out of the house or occupying herself with other tasks when she was home, which is what James and my kids had done. They helped out when they could, but they were also busy with work of various kinds. But my mom was at home all day. What was she doing with all that time?

"Mom, I just saw the state of the bathroom, and it's pretty dreadful," I told her. "Do you think you could help me clean it up a bit?"

"I'm not here to clean *your* house," she responded. "I'll get you some cleaning supplies."

"Are you serious?"

"What? Your arms aren't broken."

So, there I stood, balancing myself on my walker as I cleaned the toilet and sink for the first time in two months. My mother was nowhere to be seen.

I replayed her words in my head as I scrubbed the toothpaste and various stains off of my porcelain surfaces. I just kept thinking to myself, *Okay, so you say you're not here to clean, but what ARE you here for, then? I thought it was to help out with the things that I had trouble doing around the house, but clearly, that's not it.*

My mom made herself into more of a burden instead of a burden-reliever. She did very little to help out and made it sound like she *had* to be there. She was constantly complaining about having so much to do at her own house when she was the one who volunteered to come in the first place. She didn't have to stay; no one was forcing her to be there. I know it would've made my life a lot easier in that time if she wasn't around, even with my broken tibia.

I know the real reason why she stayed, though, even if she wouldn't admit it. She wanted everyone to think of how wonderful of a person she was for volunteering to stay with me in my time of need. I saw the looks of fake humility she made when someone found out that she was living with us.

"Oh, isn't that nice!" they'd say. "I'm sure Emma appreciates that."

"Well, she needs the help!" my mother would chuckle. "Anything I can do for my little girl."

I'm sure she thought she was being a hero, but I know that her intentions weren't nearly as pure as she made them out to be. Her narcissism caused her to be someone motivated by power and control, which was put on full display when the money started coming in after Dad had died.

Between Dad's pension, social security, and lawsuit money, he had a few different checks popping up in my mother's mailbox. I didn't ask about anything because I didn't want to beg for money and look too greedy. I also worried it would give my mother more ammo to make me look bad. I could hear her voice saying something like, "All you care about is money, Emma. You're so insensitive." I didn't want to get into all that, so I figured it was easier not to get too involved.

I remember it all being very secretive for some reason. I knew I could've pushed for more information, but I'd already done a lot of running around with legal activities, and I was tired of having to sort everything out. Plus, I remembered being in the room with Dad when he had told the lawyer that he wanted to have my mortgage paid off. It was already very hush-hush, and I didn't want to cause more trouble, so I let things go.

About a year after my father's death, my mother and I met for dinner with the lawyer who had taken care of Dad's case. We'd become close with him during the process, and it was nice to see him outside of a legal context. That said, some open ends had to be accounted for, including my unpaid mortgage. I wanted to know what had happened with all of that, but I didn't want that to be the priority. I was looking forward to a nice meal with an old friend.

We were all having a great night, and my mom eventually excused herself to use the restroom. While she was gone, the lawyer took the conversation in a different direction.

"I've been meaning to ask you something about your dad's case," he said.

"Yes, of course," I said. "What do you want to know?"

"Did you ever end up getting your mortgage paid off?"

"No, we never did."

"Ah, that's a shame," he shook his head. "Unfortunately, that kind of thing happens pretty often. It shouldn't, but it does."

"So, does that mean that we'll never have our mortgage paid off?"

"At this point, probably not. You always need to have that sort of thing in writing before anyone can take legal action."

"But I heard my dad say that those were his wishes... in front of lawyers. Even when they're witnessing what's happening, they still can't do anything about it?"

"Sadly, no. The case gets passed around to so many different people that they need to refer back to the original document that was retrieved. Word of mouth won't get you very far in this business."

I never thought I would need to have something like that in writing because there were a few different witnesses, including my mother. She heard his wishes as directly as I had heard them, but she made no effort to try to see them through. Well, that's not entirely true—she prioritized his first wish: that she'd never have to worry about anything financially. He had to die like a dog for all the money that came his way, and she ended up with all of it.

I'm sure this comes as no surprise to you, but my mortgage never got paid off.

That being said, my mother did use some of the money to help my children through college. She really did love being a grandmother, and this was a very generous thing for her to do. The optimistic side of me wants to believe that she felt guilty about my unpaid mortgage and wanted to make up for it in some way. The more cynical side of me thinks that she wanted to do it in this way specifically because it wasn't directly benefiting me. I waver between both perspectives and think both of them might be true.

But there it was: My mother, having been divorced from my father, reaping as many benefits from her ex-husband as she could just a few years after concluding those legal proceedings.

My mother claimed that the divorce was never finalized. After years of trying to gaslight me into believing that she was right, I became sick of her antics and mind games. Since divorce papers are public knowledge, I ended up contacting the court, and they sent me the papers from my parents' file. I wanted to know the truth for myself.

It was finalized. They were legally divorced. Yet, she still swears that they were never divorced, even to this day.

This was so not what I wanted to be dealing with over a year after Dad died. All I wanted was my father's ashes in a home that wouldn't require any more mortgage payments since my dad was the one to bring up that he wanted to have that covered. But, due to a seemingly endless string of loopholes and secrets, my mother tried to gain as many benefits from the situation as she could. And if it meant that I wouldn't get the thing I wanted in the process, then it would look like yet another victory for her.

From my perspective, it felt like she didn't want me to have any physical reminders of my dad. It's true that I would've thought of him every time I looked at his urn or around the home that he would've helped pay off. I don't think she wanted to have me (or anyone) yearning for him to still be with us while she was in our midst. That would've meant less attention on her, with any attention she still had being more negative or resentful. That just wouldn't do for her.

But the memories that my family had formed with my Dad could never be erased, no matter how many pictures or school projects that he helped me create were discarded. We never forgot about ice cream sodas; as long as I have anything to say about it, we never will. His legacy far surpasses the value of any physical object; I just wish we had some kind of memorabilia to honor him.

As time went on, holding my ground with my mother felt like a losing battle. But I knew that I was all of the immediate family she had left and, surely, I could never be replaced.

… Right?

Chapter 14:

The Cost of Friendship

I'm not a huge fan of small talk.

I like getting to the heart of the matter wherever I can, but that's not always an easy thing to do. I never liked entering into situations of conflict, so it was tempting for me to want to push my feelings down and say nothing. I've gotten much better at this over the years, but I found it especially difficult as a younger person. That's when I was still finding my way in the world and often feared the repercussions of challenging other opinions, especially those of authority figures. But when I found someone with whom I could be totally open and honest, I clung to those friendships as dearly as I could.

During my single years, I lived in an apartment building, as many young professionals do. I enjoyed the balance of having my own private space and meeting various people in hallways or common spaces, but those encounters were usually pretty awkward. Most of the time, any interactions that take place between two people in that context are pretty brief, if anything happens at all. Perhaps a nod or a "hello" are enough to acknowledge their existence, and that was enough. Even still, it was nice to know that people were around just so I wasn't alone. I definitely didn't expect to form a deep friendship in that environment.

I ran into my next-door neighbor on one occasion, who was a guy around my age. We went through the typical motions of "Hey, how's your day going?" "Oh, you know, same old, same old" before developing a genuine conversation from the encounter. It turned out that his name was Dale, and the two of us quickly became friends.

That friendship evolved into a sibling-type relationship that I hadn't really experienced before. Sure, I had my friendships with Amy and Carin, who felt more like sisters, but I hadn't found a brotherly connection before. There was never any romantic interest on either my end or Dale's end, but we just got along well and enjoyed one another's company. We had discovered how hard it was to make adult friends after graduating from high school, so we were just happy to have made another friend in the same building.

It didn't take long before Dale, and I started becoming a bigger part of each other's lives. We introduced each other to our respective circles of friends and did all kinds of things together in those groups. From going out to dinner to dancing in a nightclub, we ran through the whole young adult scene together with our friends. Sometimes, we went to house parties together, and at other times, we'd host parties by keeping both of our apartments open at the same time. Those were a blast. It gave us so much space to mingle in and out of each other's apartments and make sure there was something for everyone. All of our friends liked the other person.

My parents knew about our friendship as well. My dad actually got Dale a really good job at the post office he had been working at as his part-time job. Dad had to go out of his way to do it, but he didn't mind because he thought that Dale was a good guy and knew he was a close friend of mine. Dale still works at that job today and will have a great retirement package waiting for him, all thanks to my father.

But on top of sharing the same friend groups, Dale and I would spend a lot of time together in a one-on-one dynamic as well. We confided in each other about our boyfriends and girlfriends, trying to figure out who was the real deal and who was bad news (I talked to Dale about James in the early days). I could tell him about the weird dynamic I had with my mother in contrast to the ease of being with my father, and he'd be receptive to everything I was saying. And we'd bond over a lot of general life stuff, too, from figuring out how to be an adult to figuring out the purpose of our own life. We were just two big kids trying to find our way, and it felt like we had a sibling to help us through it. I can credit a lot of my appreciation for deeper conversations to the chats I used to have with Dale.

Even after we moved out of the building, Dale and I continued to stay in touch. As the years went by, we both got married and attended each other's weddings. We both had kids and would take our children for playdates with one another. Our spouses got to know each other as well, and it blossomed into a true family friendship. I felt so grateful that a simple chat with the person living in the neighboring apartment grew into such a unique connection.

Several years after my father had passed, my mother was having a medical procedure done. While she was recovering, I was taking care of all the paperwork and logistical arrangements. This was actually one time when I felt that it was reasonable for my mother to be doted on; she was already going through a lot of physical stress from this procedure, and I wanted to help make her life easier. I was her only family member in the area, immediate or extended, so it just made sense that I would help out.

Anyways, I left the hospital while she was recovering to get some of the insurance papers that the medical staff had requested. It required me to go into her file and retrieve some personal information, just in case something unexpected should happen. That meant rummaging a few papers around and stumbling upon her life insurance policy. As I was pulling the papers, my eyes caught something noteworthy.

She had her beneficiary listed as "Dale."

I had to do a double-take. Still Dale. I couldn't believe my eyes. And because his social security number was recorded on that file, that meant that he had to know about it, too.

There was no way he couldn't know. How else would she be able to get such private information? He was smart enough to know that he shouldn't just give that number out freely. She must've asked for it, and he must've been aware of what was happening.

I felt sick to my stomach. How could they sneak around behind my back like this?

Well, for my mom, this didn't feel too different from her previous actions. It's sad to say that, but it was true. It had become a habit at this point. She wouldn't tell me about something while it was happening, only to leave me having to discover it long after everything had been settled. That's what happened with my dad's ashes; that's what happened with my childhood memories; that's what happened with Tucker. I could go on, but that paints a pretty clear picture already. I still tried to hold onto the hope that she wanted to come clean with all of her secrets, but I would be the only one who ended up getting burned.

My mother's betrayal still hurt, but I had grown accustomed to it. What really hurt was Dale's involvement in the situation. He was one of my best friends. He knew better than most people how badly my mother had hurt me over the years. And this wasn't just some favor that he was helping my mom with... this was her life insurance policy! If anything were to happen to her, everything would go to him, not her own daughter. It would be one thing if she offered this to him, but he had to agree to it, too. And by doing so, he would be intentionally separating a family. Even with all of the crap that my mother and I had gone through, we were still a family. It was so inappropriate for him to meddle in any family dynamic that wasn't his own, never mind when it was with me.

I sat on that information for a long time. As enraged as I was about the situation, I knew I couldn't bring it up while my mom was still in the hospital. She needed to have a proper recovery and didn't need any unnecessary distractions to hamper that. Plus, I wanted her to be in full fighting strength by the time I confronted her and Dale on it, because I was definitely planning on doing so.

I kept it in for as long as I could, but when I finally had Dale and my mother in the same room together, I knew it was my golden opportunity.

"So, is there anything you two want to tell me, or should I start asking you questions?" I began.

Their eyes widened as they looked at each other, but they paused for a moment before speaking.

"We're not sure what you mean," Dale hesitated. "What are you getting at?"

"Don't speak for her, Dale," I said. The fact that he had said "we" already told me he knew what I was talking about, but he wasn't brave enough to say it. I figured I'd let my mother have a turn. "Mom? Is there anything you want to tell me about you and Dale? Last chance."

"You're talking nonsense again," my mother said. "There's nothing to tell."

Nope. Not today.

"You've got some nerve trying to smooth everything over," I said. "I know about your life insurance policy, Mom. I know that Dale is your beneficiary. I had to get your papers ready while you were in the hospital, and I saw his name in your file. It was right there, plain as day. Were you—either of you—ever gonna tell me about this?!"

"No, it's not like that!" Dale started getting defensive. "I wouldn't be taking anything away from you, obviously. You're her daughter."

"Yet, it's *your* name written on the insurance form," I retorted. "How do you explain that, Dale? Does that mean you're gonna be in charge of her funeral when that day comes?"

"Em, I would never betray you," Dale panicked. "You know this about me by now. I really don't know what you're talking about."

"Then why does she have your social security number?" I fired back. "You knew that this would cheat me out of her insurance policy, and yet you did it anyway!"

"Why are you so keen on getting my things after I die, Emma?" my mother chimed in. "You didn't do anything to earn it, so why should you be entitled to that?"

"Oh, I don't know, Mom, maybe because I'm your daughter? The only immediate family member you have who can barely tolerate you? Did you ever think that I might be worth talking to about this?"

"Sounds to me like you'd rather have me dead than alive. You're impossible to reason with."

"*You're* impossible to reason with! Every time I try to do something nice for you, you just find a way to cut me down even further. Why can't you just admit that you went behind my back to make Dale your beneficiary? It's already there in writing; you may as well just admit it!"

"There's nothing that I need to admit, and I don't care for your attitude."

"You're one to talk!" I turned my attention to Dale. "And you. Why? In all the years that we've been friends, you've known better than almost anyone what this means to me. Are you happy? Are you happy knowing that you've ruined our friendship?"

Dale's voice got very quiet. "I didn't think you cared about money so much."

"Are you kidding me? Why are you taking *her* side?! What has she ever done for you?!"

"That's enough, Emma," my mother said. "Your immature temper tantrums have gone far enough. There's nothing to tell, and what's done is done."

It wasn't a pleasant conversation, to say the least.

Both Dale and my mother denied my allegations profusely. I know what I saw. I wasn't willing to fold on this issue because I value the truth. Apparently, they didn't feel the same way.

My father would've been so disappointed in Dale. After pulling all those strings, Dad wanted to make sure that Dale would be okay, but Dale completely took advantage of that. In spite of being set up with a great job for the rest of his life, it still wasn't enough for Dale. He wanted more. Some people just seem to be perpetually greedy and never satisfied.

Since that incident, Dale and I haven't spoken, and I certainly have no plans of reaching out to him now. It would hurt too much. He and my mom have become quite close. He sure was quick to go to my mother's house after my father died to collect some of his belongings. I'm sure he has been like the son that she never had.

I never believed that he would be capable of this. The guy I lived next to was a hard worker who wanted to earn a living for himself. I never would've pegged him for the guy to try to put those who were closest to him down to get himself ahead. But I suppose money and possessions, and status can bring out someone's impure motivations. Those things change us, which is why I'm thankful to live a fairly modest life.

I never wanted to be my mother's beneficiary because I would become filthy rich, but because I thought it was the honorable thing to do for your only child. But this event cemented for me that my mother really didn't want to see me in that way. The only thing that gives me peace is knowing that Dale will have to live with the consequences of his choices. Every day that he has to walk into his job, he knows that my father got it for him. When he gets those life insurance payments, he has to remember what it cost him. As for me, my conscience is clear.

Of course, he can't be the only one to blame. It takes two to tango. As I said earlier, this kind of behavior was no longer surprising coming from my mom, although it still packed a vicious punch. Every time I thought I'd learned everything there was to know about her, she'd still find a way to surprise me with something else. Yet another victory for her, I suppose.

I guess you can never really know someone. Not fully, anyway. That's what I learned through this whole experience with Dale. I realized where my mother's loyalties lied and tried to accept that she refused to see me as the daughter she'd always wanted.

I had no idea why that was the case. But a phone call I received many years later changed my perception of the meaning of family forever.

The Phone Call

.

Chapter 15:

Call Waiting

It was a Friday afternoon in June.

I was basking in a typical summer day in the Northeast—sun shining down, warming every pore on my skin as the robins and goldfinches trill into the open air. I loved the early signs of summer emerging after another long and chilly winter. They breathed so much life into Connecticut that I wanted to embrace the new season ahead. Plus, few feelings are quite as freeing for anyone living in a colder part of the world as stepping outside without a jacket for the first time in several months. Life was good.

As a way to make the most of these summer months in particular, I'd made it a habit to go out for daily walks. It reminded me of being a child again and wanting to be outside for as much as I could. I loved the milder summers we got in the Northeast; the air was crisp and rejuvenating, and we could stay outside for a while without sweating buckets. And walking was a great way for me to clear my head from the day-to-day responsibilities of life. It was time that I took for myself to take a break from the other tasks I had going on that day.

As a way to make the most of this "me time," I tended to spend my walks catching up with various people over the phone. A walk was the perfect amount of time to do that, and depending on how short the conversations were, I could make room for a few different catch-ups on the same walk. It was also a great way to squeeze in a bit of light exercise since walking and talking at the same time is surprisingly tiring. If I was talking to someone and reached a hill, though, it turned into moderate exercise.

The first person on my list of people to call would always be my mother. I knew that talking to her wasn't the most relaxing thing I could be doing in my free time, but I'd actually gotten into a pretty good habit of doing it. For starters, it put a time limit on the conversations, which would have to end by the time I arrived back home, if not earlier. On top of that, it also cleared my conscience of knowing that I'd done my due diligence in keeping in touch with my mother. If I didn't call her during those walks, then I'd feel guilty every time I wasn't talking with her. I'd get myself stressed out trying to think of a good time to call her, and it just wouldn't have been worth it. Such is the obligation of an only child with a widowed mother.

On this particular Friday, I was out for my daily walk, and after a few minutes, I decided to give my mother a ring.

"Hello?" she said.

"Hi, Mom."

"Hi, Emma."

"I'm just out for a walk, so I figured I'd call. How are things?"

"Oh, fine. Same old. I went to a new lunch spot the other day that had pretty good food."

"Oh, that's nice. I'm glad you're able to check out some of the new restaurants in town."

"Yeah, it was good."

"Have you heard back about your next appointment yet?"

"Not yet, but I'll let you know when I do so that you can come over."

"Sure, that sounds good."

"How are the kids?"

"They're doing really well. School and extracurriculars are keeping them busy, but we check in with them from time to time."

"That's good. Glad to hear it."

"Yeah, they're really loving it."

Pretty standard fare for the two of us. The two of us were on the phone for a while, chatting about this and that. I don't remember everything that came up during that conversation, but I do remember where things eventually went.

"James is doing well, I take it?"

"Oh, yeah, he's great. Very busy, working lots of hours. The guys at work actually told him the other day—"

"Hold on, Emma. I'm getting another call. Could you hold on for a sec?"

"Okay, yeah, sure."

My mom put me on hold as she took the other call. This would happen on occasion since she had various friends and family members checking in with her more regularly after Dad died. Even if my mother was a pill to deal with at times, she really did have a great community around her. They were always great to me, too. I don't think her friends and family members knew every little thing happening in our household growing up, but they knew enough about my mother to know that it wasn't always easy for me. They looked out for me while still maintaining a relationship with her, which I appreciated.

Anyways, I figured that a relative or friend of hers had given her a call. Usually, she'd tell them that she'd call them back and finish her conversation with me, or if it was urgent, she'd tell me that she had to take the call, and then we'd hang up. But either way, she made sure to get back to me and let me know what was going on.

So, I stayed on the line and waited for her to come back.

And I kept waiting.

And waiting.

I turned a new corner on my walk.

I waited.

And waited.

"Mom, are you there?"

Still nothing.

I kept waiting.

Waiting.

Waiting.

A few minutes had passed, and I hadn't heard a peep from my mom. I found it a bit unusual because she'd never done this before, but I also didn't think too much of it. She wouldn't have forgotten to call me back. A small part of me wondered if something had happened to her, but she seemed fine to me. There was nothing worrisome about her tone of voice that would've suggested any issues on her end.

Everything is probably fine, I thought to myself. *She probably just got caught up in whatever conversation kept happening. Carry on. She'll call back when she's free.*

After giving it a few more minutes, I figured I'd move on.

"Hey, Mom, I don't know if you can hear me, but I'm gonna hang up now. Let me know if you need anything. I'll talk to you later," I spoke into a void, just on the off chance that she could hear me.

I hung up the phone and proceeded to call the next person on my list. I'd periodically check my home screen to see if my mother was trying to call me back, but I never got a notification for an incoming call.

I got home at the end of my walk. No incoming calls.

I started on some chores. Nothing.

As it got to be dinner time, I started to think this was strange. Several hours had passed by this point, and I hadn't heard anything from my mother. She always called back. I tried not to think about it too much, but I couldn't help myself.

Is she okay? I thought. *Maybe she got a call from her doctor or something. I hope she wouldn't leave me in suspense for too long if she got some bad news. No, she wouldn't do that to her own daughter, would she?*

In this technological age we live in, it's so easy to take communication for granted. We're so accustomed to giving someone a call or sending them a text or an email, and it's weird when we don't hear from those same people by an expected time. In a way, it almost felt easier when I was young because there was no expectation of having to stay in contact with my parents; I just had to be home by curfew. But now, we have an embarrassment of riches when it comes to methods of communication, which also brings the expectation of having to stay connected all the time. It can be exhausting at times, but when we're disconnected from someone, it can almost cause more anxiety if it's beyond the norm.

That's how it felt when I didn't hear back from my mother. I had grown so used to her reaching out to me after getting interrupted by another call that I was waiting for her to call me back, and it made me nervous when I didn't hear from her. She was still my mother, after all. I wanted to make sure that she was okay.

But before I got too far ahead of myself, I dialed her again in the evening, hoping she would pick up.

Ring...

Ring...

Ri—

"Hello?"

"Mom?"

"Hi, Emma."

"Are you okay?"

"Things are... Yeah, I'm fine."

I thought that was a bit of a weird answer, but I went with it.

"Okay, well, thank goodness. You didn't call me back after taking that other call this afternoon, so I was starting to get a bit worried."

"Yeah, that took... longer than expected."

"Why didn't you call back?"

She paused.

"Mom?"

"It's complicated."

"Are you sure you're okay?"

"Emma, I'm fine."

"I'm sorry; I don't mean to make you feel bad, but I just want to make sure everything is okay."

"And it is."

"Okay..."

Silence. Awkward silence. But curiosity was getting the better of me. Perhaps it was because she hadn't called me back this afternoon, but I felt like I could ask her about the phone call.

"Mom, is it okay if I ask what the call was about?"

"It's too hard to explain over the phone."

"Well, I have time—"

"I need to tell you about it in person."

Whoa. That was the last thing I was expecting to hear her say. My mom wanted to spend time with me? Willingly? Outside of holidays or major milestones for the kids? This had to be a huge piece of news.

"You… Okay, um… Yeah, okay. When were you thinking?"

"I don't know, one sec… I have a few things on the calendar that I can't miss over the next few days… So, I won't be able to come until Tuesday."

And wait four more days to hear about it? No way. That was way too far away. Now that I knew she had this massive thing to tell me, I wanted to hear about it as soon as possible.

"What? Tuesday? Mom, if it's that important, you can just tell me now. I'm not doing anything."

"No, this can't be done on the phone."

"But Mom, it's a 120-mile drive for you to get here."

"I know. I've made the drive before."

"Well, I know that, but I'm saying that you don't have to make the drive here if you don't want to. It's a long way for you to go, and I have the time now. I could even go to you— Wait, no, never mind. I have stuff going on at work that I can't put aside. Shoot."

"No. Just stay there."

"Are you sure you can't tell me now?"

"No. Not now."

"But why can't—"

"I said no, Emma."

Another pause. She had made up her mind. I knew there was no budging her opinion, so I figured I might as well acknowledge the new plan.

"So, Tuesday, then?"

"Yeah. I'll let you know when I'm leaving."

"Okay. Do you wanna stay over?"

"No, that won't be necessary."

"Are you sure? 'Cause you're welcome to—"

"I'll see you on Tuesday, Emma."

"Okay. See you on Tuesday."

"Bye."

"Bye."

I went to tap the little red circle on my phone, but she beat me to it. The call ended.

I sat down, feeling a bit stunned at everything that had just happened. I never expected to get that kind of answer (which had really left more questions than answers at this point). What did she have to tell me? And why did it have to wait until Tuesday? I had no idea what to think. I didn't want to be kept in suspense for four more days, but I didn't have any other choice.

So, I just had to wait.

It was the longest four days of my life. I don't know if I got anything done during that time. I must've done something, but I felt like I was staring at the clock the whole time. I could barely concentrate on anything because I was so hung up on what my mother had to tell me. It felt like time was going by more slowly, specifically because I wanted it to go by faster. I couldn't sit still. I had to know what was going on.

But alas, Tuesday finally came around. I was nervous, even though I didn't really have anything to be nervous about; my mom was the one with the big news. Even still, I was on edge. I didn't know if this would affect me or my family in some way, but I was more disturbed by the way this news had changed my mother's demeanor. She had never behaved this way before. Sure, she'd try to put off things that made her uncomfortable in the past, but this time felt different. She seemed less emotional about the situation and more matter-of-fact as if this was the way things had to be done. Honestly, this was a bit off-putting after witnessing 54 years of her volatile emotional outbursts.

I tried not to hover by the front door, but I kept my eye out to see her car pull into my driveway. After seeing her car, I turned around and paced around the room until I heard her come to the door. Once she knocked, I took a deep breath before opening it.

"Hi, Mom. Was the drive okay?"

"It was fine."

I took a step back to let her get settled in, but she quickly started walking toward the kitchen. I kept pace with her and tried to make her feel comfortable.

"Have a seat, Mom."

I pulled out a chair for myself but noticed that my mother kept standing. She kept staring toward the floor as her fingers wiggled by her thighs. I had never seen her like this before. She was always the tough one in a given situation; things just wouldn't get to her. The only time I could remember her being rattled was when the robbers came into our store in Enfield, but she was far more nervous here.

"Mom? Do you wanna sit?"

"No."

It wasn't worth pushing it. I dragged my chair closer to the table and rested my hands in front of me, gesturing to my mom that she could speak when she was ready. She never made eye contact with me as she spoke, so I leaned in a bit closer to make sure I heard everything.

"So, when you and I were talking, I got a call from another woman," my mom began. She took a deep breath before saying her next line.

"I didn't recognize her voice at first but stayed on the line anyway. She asked me if I was Doris Nasato. I said yes. Then, she asked me if I'd put a baby up for adoption in 1961... and I said yes."

I just stared at her for a minute. I didn't think I'd heard her correctly. If she had a baby before me...

Then, it registered. I thought I knew what she was getting at, but I had to ask it out loud, just to make sure.

"So... was that... was she... your daughter?"

"... Yes."

"So… does that mean…"

"Yes. You have a sister."

Chapter 16:

Janet

I was shocked but stayed as calm as I could.

I couldn't process everything quickly enough to have an emotional reaction. It felt like I'd been stunned. I honestly didn't know how to feel about it at first. I certainly wasn't expecting to find out I had a sister at 54 years old.

But there you go.

I'm not an only child.

I now understood why my mother wanted to wait until she met with me in person to drop this massive piece of news. There was so much to digest, and my mind flooded with questions. I'm thankful that my emotions took a second to get caught up so that the rational part of my brain had a second to address some of those questions.

"Wow, okay..." I began. "What's her name?"

"Janet."

"Janet, okay..." I know that asking about her name didn't really accomplish much, but it was the first thing that came to my head. But I couldn't just leave it at that. "So... you just found out who she was when she called?"

"Yeah," my mother said. "I never had any contact with her before that."

"Okay... How did she find out... or find you, I guess?"

"The ancestry kits."

"Ohhh..."

A few Christmases before this, I'd gotten the whole family a kit where we could send in a small DNA sample and use those results to discover more about our heritage. It was a neat little experiment to learn more about where we came from and the members of our family line. Looking back, though, I'm surprised my mother agreed to keep the gift, knowing that this could've resulted from it.

"So, how would that work then?" I asked. "Would our family lineage be out there so she could find you?"

"Something like that. I guess they're allowed to publicize a certain amount of information from their database that gave her enough to track me down. She must've found my number after that."

"Okay, that makes sense…"

I hesitated to ask the question that I'm sure my mother was dreading, but I couldn't put it off any longer. I had to know.

"So… what happened?"

My mother took a deep sigh, still refusing to make eye contact with me as she spoke. "When your father was in Vietnam, I was… I got lonely. It was so hard to be away from him. We were in the early years of our marriage, and I didn't know how he was doing or if he was even alive. I knew he wouldn't have been deployed or even a member of the Air Force if he wasn't ready, but… I was scared."

I hung onto every word. This was all so much to take in. I pressed my hands firmly against the table to try and cover up the fact that my hands were sweating.

"So, I would go out," she continued, "just trying to keep myself around people so I didn't have to be reminded of how worried I was. And then, I met Vincent."

She gripped the top of the chair she was leaning on a bit tighter.

"He was sweet… charming… a little dangerous… and knew exactly what to say. He was a sweet-talking, good-for-nothing scoundrel, and I ate it up. I brought him home with me, and he stayed the night."

You could hear a pin drop; the room was so quiet.

"A few months later, I found out I was pregnant, so I gave him a call to break the news. I was terrified. I didn't even know his last name, and here I was, about to have his baby. He told me he didn't want anything to do with it. I panicked. I didn't know what to do. So… I had the baby while your father was away, put her up for adoption, and her new family took her… and I never saw Vincent or my baby again."

At this point, I couldn't help but wonder what would've happened if Vincent *did* want to be involved. Would she have left my father? While he was at war? I knew it was no use to speculate on that too much since it didn't end up happening, but I couldn't help it. I was curious. After seeing the way that my mother had treated Dad for so many years, I wondered if she felt resentful for having to "settle" for her second family. Maybe that would explain why she'd taken her anger out on us for all that time.

To this day, I don't believe her story. Parts of it may be true, but I know there's more to the story than I was told. That's the thing about being in such close quarters with a narcissist for 50 years—it's hard to know when they're telling the truth, especially when they're describing a situation that could make them look bad. They love attention, but in order to keep that attention, they have to be liked to a certain degree, and this kind of story would severely threaten that. I think she was covering up for someone or something in the account she gave me, although I have no physical proof of that. Just years of lived experience.

And while I can share my curiosities with you, I don't think I'll ever find out the full truth. I'm pretty sure she'll take that to her grave. She'll be the only person to ever know who the real father of her first baby was.

For the first time, I remember feeling glad that my father was dead. I don't know what would've happened if he ever had to live through this. I'd never seen him get angry with my mother before, but he also never needed to address news of this magnitude before. I don't know if he ever knew about the other affair she was having with the guy from Hartford, but even if he did, he never had to see it. It would've been different from having to confront the child that his wife had with another man while he was serving overseas. Even though it wasn't the child's fault, it would've been a gut-wrenching situation for my father. I'm just thankful he never had to go through that.

After my mom finished sharing her story, I just sat in silence. I didn't really know what to say, and there wasn't a whole lot more that she wanted to say. We both just needed time to process everything.

"I think I'm gonna head out," my mother said through a sigh. "I don't want to be here when your husband and children come home. I'd rather you tell them about it, not me."

"Are you sure? It's a long way for you to drive—"

"I'll be fine."

I didn't question her again. I didn't really want her to stay because I needed space to properly react to everything without her around, but I felt obligated to ask at least once. I was a little bit relieved when she turned me down.

"Okay, well, drive safe," I said. "Let me know when you get home."

"I will," she said as we made our way to the front door. She fiddled with her keys and rested her hand on the doorknob but paused before opening the door. "I'm going to have to put Janet and her family into my will now…"

With that, she opened the door, got in her car, and made the 120-mile journey back home after a five-minute conversation with me.

As I watched her drive away, I wrestled with that last comment she made. Write Janet into her will? My mother had given this woman up for adoption 56 years ago. She knew nothing about her and had only heard from her for the first time four days ago; the two of them hadn't even met in person. And now, she's already talking about putting her into her will?

I found it all to be a bit strange, both the sentiment and the fact that she made the comment at all. My mother clearly didn't want to stay to have the rest of that conversation, yet she felt compelled to drop that remark in before she left. Weird. But I let it roll off since I was still in a state of shock from everything I'd just heard. I wasn't really sure what to make of any of it and was left in an empty house to try to understand some of it.

I'm glad there was a period when I had the house to myself because I needed that time to figure out what to feel. Although I had good reason to feel angry about the situation, I actually didn't feel as upset as I could've felt. I was definitely thrown off by it, but the surprise I felt was actually a lot more positive. My mother just had a vulnerable moment with me, and I now had a sister in my life. Oh my gosh. I had a sister! This was huge news, and I had to tell my family about it.

I was relieved to see James and my children come through the door after work and school, respectively. As soon as they walked through the door, I told them, "We need to have an important family meeting tonight." They could sense that this "meeting" was an urgent matter. Thankfully, they were very quick to go with the flow.

They all took it pretty well. It's unsurprising to me; they're all very welcoming people. I was a bit nervous to tell them just because I didn't know exactly how they'd react, but I knew they'd be very gracious about the whole thing. My youngest child probably had the best reaction out of everyone. Usually, my children are good at playing off of the reactions of other people before they put their own feelings out there, but my youngest child could not contain it. My oldest child managed to sneak in a picture of the expression. Absolute shock and awe. It's pretty comical; I won't lie.

Once we had our laughs, I knew I had to address how we were to go forward from here. Since I was the biological bridge between my family and my mother, I felt a sense of responsibility to make sure everyone was still on good terms with one another.

"So, now that you guys know, would you be okay with calling Grandma at some point and letting her know that you're okay with this?" I asked them.

They all look at each other, nodding their heads. "Yeah, we'd be okay with that."

They're so great. I love them.

James and my children all took turns calling my mom to have their conversation with her. I wasn't around to listen to the whole chat, but I picked up bits and pieces. At one point, I remember hearing my husband say, "Grandma, you've been a bad girl!"

We all had a good laugh about it. That was very much the tone of those conversations because that's how we all felt about the situation. It happened 56 years ago. Why agonize over it now?

I'm sure my mother really appreciated having those moments with my family. It took a huge act of courage for her to break that news to me because, if she'd had it her way, I probably never would've found out. But to know that the story was out there and my family still loved her would've meant the world to her.

We slowly broke the news to other people in our circles when the timing was appropriate. Many people told me that they were surprised at how accepting I was of the situation.

"I don't know how you're so okay with this," they'd say. "If it were me, I'd be furious. I don't know if I could do it. How lucky your mother is to have a daughter like you and a family that all feels the same way about it."

I don't want to toot my own horn, but it meant a lot that they recognized what a big deal it was to come to terms with this. It was huge news. I know my mother and I had a rocky relationship over the years, and if I wanted to, I could've absolutely gone off on her and severed the relationship forever. But what would that have accomplished? It just would've torn our family apart, and I didn't want my kids to be without their grandmother because of a grudge I might've had with her. That wasn't worth it to me. If there was a way to move forward by incorporating this new element, then I was more than willing to pursue that option.

Plus, as I said, Janet was the result of a one-night stand 56 years ago. Was I really in a place to punish someone permanently based on one thing they did before I was even around to say anything about it? In some cases, perhaps that would be enough. I know that my relationship with Dale will never be the same because we immediately stopped talking on a permanent basis after years of friendship. To me, that's different from this situation. If he's unwilling to mend the relationship, then I don't see a purpose in expending too much of my energy trying to repair that.

But regardless of whatever my mom was going through, she still had me. Getting pregnant with Janet didn't deter her from staying with my dad; granted, Vincent didn't really leave her with much of a choice, but she still stuck it out. It definitely helped explain some of her behavior over the years. I could now partially understand why she took things out on me the way she did since she was acting from a place of pain. But what really hit me was the realization of why she always loved babies so much, especially her grandbabies—she didn't get to keep one of her own. The pain of letting Janet go that day must've stuck with her (how could it not?), so when she held another baby in her arms, she cherished those moments as much as she could. In that way, I found this whole revelation to be a huge blessing. Even if I didn't agree with the things she said or did, I at least had a better sense of why she said or did those things.

Plus—and I think this is the greatest news of all—I gained a sister through all of this. I'd dreamed of how amazing that might've been ever since I became friends with Amy and later with Carin. But now, it was a reality. For the first time in my life, I had a real, biological sibling who also just happened to be a sister. How amazing was that? Most of my friends had siblings, and now, I have one, too. It was so exciting to say that.

Admittedly, I had a good deal of shock over the situation, but I tried to see it as more of a celebration than a loss. When my friends started hearing about the situation, they were quick to say, "Janet sure got the better end of that deal." They knew what my mother was like when I was growing up and were quick to be on my side. I'd just shrug it off by saying, "Well, she told my mother that she'd had a pretty good life, so I guess it all worked out."

It was an easy way to handle those kinds of comments, although they did cause me to imagine how Janet's life had turned out. What was she like? What was her adopted family like? How did she decide to find my mother?

But before I got too far ahead of myself, I knew that I eventually had to meet her. Now that Janet had made the first move, my mom would have to reciprocate in some way, and it would just be a matter of time before I got involved as well. It ended up being sooner than I'd expected.

Chapter 17:

The First Meeting

A few days after the announcement, my mother rapidly tried to figure out the next steps.

"Well, we'll have to meet her at some point," she said, "and I'd rather do it sooner than later. So, when are you free?"

Honestly, I was caught off guard by her question. It wasn't that I didn't want to meet Janet, but this was still so new to me. I hadn't fully wrapped my head around the idea of having a sister in the first place. And until that happened, I didn't know if I was ready to come face-to-face with her so quickly after discovering that. I was more than willing to do it, but I didn't think it would be fair to anyone to be in a state of shock while doing it.

"Wait, you want me to come?" I asked my mom.

"Well, yeah," she said. "Don't you want to?"

"Yeah, I do, eventually... I don't know; I mean, she's *your* daughter. You've known about her way longer than I have. She's expecting you, but she's not necessarily expecting me. Don't you think you should go by yourself first?"

"I don't understand. Why don't you wanna meet her?"

"It's not that I don't want to meet her, Mom. But you've been waiting for this moment for 56 years, and I just found out about her existence a few days ago. This is a huge moment for you, and it doesn't seem right for me to take that away from you by being there." I hoped that phrasing it in that way would make it seem like I would be a liability if I went to that first meeting. It didn't go as planned.

"Well, not really. I just found out about her existence a few days ago, too. Sure, I knew I had another daughter, but I didn't think I'd ever see her again."

"But that's why this is such a huge deal. You're being reunited after 56 years apart—that's longer than I've even been alive. Tell you what: If things go well between the two of you, I'd be more than happy to go to the next meeting because I assume there'd be another one. But I don't want to throw anything off by being there the first time you come face-to-face with your daughter."

"Why do you insist on making things difficult, Emma?"

"I'm not trying to be difficult, but I'm just saying that it doesn't make sense for me to be at that first meeting. It's not about me. It's about you and Janet."

"Stop being a softie and just tell me when you're free."

"All I'm saying is… Why don't you go by yourself first to meet with her and get whatever needs to be said off of your chest, and then, when everyone's on the same page, I can come for the next meeting."

"No, I don't wanna do that. You're gonna come with me when I meet with her."

"Are you sure? And I mean, really sure?"

"Are you trying to screw with me or something? You're going. End of story."

She kept applying more pressure on me, which made me feel more and more trapped. I tried desperately to find a way out despite feeling further away from that escape door.

"I still don't know if I feel comfortable with going to that first meeting, though. Janet's your daughter."

"And she's your sister, so you'd better get used to it. We'll go on a Saturday."

"*This* Saturday?!"

"No, will you relax? Next weekend is a holiday weekend. We'll grab dinner next Saturday. We'll carpool."

And I slowly began to accept that the door was officially closing.

"Uhh, alright… Where do you wanna go?"

"I don't know yet. I'll figure it out and let you know."

"Okay."

I found it so ironic that the one time I didn't want to do something with my mother, she wouldn't let me say no. Ordinarily, she would've come up with an excuse to have me avoid joining her to do something unless she wanted to come with me on her own terms. I hated that I caved to her yet again because I still felt this weird mixture of pressure and guilt to have to say "yes" to her demands, even as a grown woman. Her demand was to force me into a first meeting that had very little to do with me, and I felt like I was gonna be the awkward third wheel.

Oh, NOW you want to spend time with me, I thought to myself. *Why now?*

Honestly, I think she was scared. She'd never admit that to me, but I think was riddled with fear. How couldn't she be? There was no way of knowing how Janet would react to her. From Janet's perspective, this was the woman who gave her up when she was born. There was no telling as to what kind of person she ended up becoming—she could've been well-adjusted, or she could've been brimming with resentment. So, I think my mother wanted to have moral support and strength in numbers by having me go with her. I don't know how much she valued my opinion, but I believe the thought of having me physically there with her made her feel less alone.

As awkward as I felt doing it, I could understand where she was coming from. It's nerve-wracking to have to walk into a new situation by yourself. Even if you're not very close with someone, it's reassuring to know that you're not the only person there. Did I feel like I was a tool being used to her own ends? Yeah, a little bit. But did I also feel like she genuinely wanted to have the loving support of a family member with her, who could also evaluate the character of this new woman? Yeah, I do.

So, I reluctantly agreed to go with her, and my daughter ended up coming with us as well. We did end up going on the Saturday of a holiday weekend, with my daughter and I driving about 90 miles until we met up with my mom at a mall. Then, the three of us drove together for another 15 minutes to the restaurant where we'd be meeting Janet.

My husband decided that he would sit this one out and let the girls go together. I was a little jealous. A part of me wanted to ask if I could stay back with him, but I held back on the off-chance the comment made its way to my mother's ears. I wanted my mother to be in as good a mood as possible heading into that dinner without any sneaking suspicion that I was somehow trying to sabotage this for her.

The three of us arrived at the restaurant first, so we got ourselves seated at our table and waited for Janet to arrive. My daughter and I tried to engage in a bit of small talk to pass the time (although I'm not a huge fan of it, it felt like the better option compared to sitting in anxious silence). My mother would say something from time to time, but her eyes were glued to the door. Then, something struck me.

"Mom, do you know what Janet looks like?" I asked my mother.

"Not exactly," she said, barely moving her eyes. "She described a few of her physical features to me, but I haven't seen any pictures of her or anything."

"Well, I guess she has the name of the reservation, so I'm sure it'll be fine," I added. "I'm thankful the drive up here was pretty smooth. I can't remember—"

My mother abruptly stood up, letting the backs of her legs push her chair further behind her. My daughter and I turned our heads toward the door, and I'll admit, my heart started beating more quickly.

A woman walked through the door who looked identical to my mother.

It was a bit eerie. It truly felt like I was looking at my mother roughly 20 years ago. She looked so familiar, despite having never met her before this moment.

When the woman's eyes met my mother's, I could tell that she was a bit spooked, but she didn't make it look like she was totally rattled. After the hostess escorted her to our table, the woman waited for a second or two before speaking.

"You must be Doris," she said to my mom.

"I am," my mother responded.

A brief pause ensued.

"Well, I wouldn't have bothered obsessing over myself in the mirror this afternoon if I already knew what I was going to look like!"

We all chuckled at her light-hearted remark, breathing a small sigh of relief.

"In case there was any doubt, I'm Janet," she confirmed.

"Janet, this is my other daughter, Emma, and my granddaughter," my mother introduced us, and everyone hugged.

Janet had also come with her family, namely her children, their spouses, and her grandchildren. I suppose my mother had told her that she was bringing me, which gave Janet some incentive to bring her family as well. We all took our seats and began a long-awaited conversation.

As much as I'd like to tell you that it was some dramatic occasion like one you'd see on television, it really wasn't that at all. I know that might not make for the most entertaining story, but it was a very pleasant and tame meal. It was just like any other dinner that you'd come across between a group of people who were meeting each other for the first time. It was actually a lot less awkward than a few first dates I'd been on because we didn't have to worry about "where this was going." There was no pretense for that. We knew that we were in each other's lives now, and it was time to catch up on everything that had happened over the last 50-some-odd years.

Janet shared her life very openly. She was quite vulnerable about everything she'd gone through mentally regarding my mother, but she presented everything from a place of curiosity. It was more of an "I wonder what happened to her" situation instead of a "How could she do this to me" perspective. There was never any hint of malice coming from her, which was honestly really refreshing. She really just wanted to reconnect with the woman who'd given birth to her.

She also mentioned how she got in contact with my mother, which repeated parts of the story that my mother had already told us. Janet was able to find my mom through the publicized ancestry information and tracked down her address and phone number from there. It was such a neat little story, although it prompted a rather interesting comment from my mother.

"Well, I have to tell ya… After Emma's father died, I hired a private investigator to try and find you!"

"Oh really?" Janet responded. "That's fascinating."

"Yeah, but he came up empty. Couldn't find a thing. But there was nothing holding me back from at least trying to look for you, so I kept looking. I guess you beat me to it!"

That was… bizarre, I thought to myself. *So many secrets…*

That whole exchange was peculiar to me. First of all, my mother has never, ever been so bubbly about anyone "beating" her at anything. Maybe that was a way for her to pretend she didn't care about the situation when she really did. I still don't know that for sure, but it struck me as odd at the time. In fact, her whole attitude that night was different from how I'd seen her act before. I tried not to think too much of it because I knew that this was a big night for her, but it was something I wanted to remember for going forward.

But the other, more significant portion of that fact was how blatantly she'd disregarded me in the situation. I understood that revealing Janet to my father would've had more significant implications for him than it would for me. I got that. But it still would've been nice for her to acknowledge Janet and the situation with me before she tried looking for her behind my back. Maybe I'm reacting unfairly about it now, but I also just didn't like how everything was hidden for so long. I would've helped her look for Janet if I'd known about it earlier; it would've still taken some getting used to in those early stages, but I'd want our family to be reunited. But there wasn't a peep about it until there had to be.

It was all very strange, but I tried not to dwell on it too much during the night.

All in all, the evening was great. Although I still think that the first meeting should've just been between Janet and my mother, things ended up working out well. The conversation flowed freely, and there weren't any awkward moments, either. It was just that one comment that hit my ears a bit funny, but that had nothing to do with Janet or her family. That was just my mother being my mother, and I'd come to expect that she'd throw something out of left field like that. Janet and her family were amazing from the start. All of them were such warm and friendly people, and the thought of expanding our family to include them was a wonderful prospect.

But the most bewildering thing to me continued to be the resemblance between my mother and Janet. I couldn't stop my eyes from darting back and forth between the two of them. They looked like twins, which was the opposite of me and my mom. I look nothing like her. As a matter of fact, I've had it confirmed to me multiple times over the years from my mother directly.

"You don't look anything like me," she'd whine. "I always wished I had a little girl who looked exactly like me. You don't even like the same things as me. It makes me sad to think that you don't wish you could look more like your mother."

I don't know what would get her so upset. It wasn't my fault that I had certain features, but she made it out to be like it was a huge problem. And we did like different things. I do favor my dad's side in more ways than one. I look a lot like his mother, which I am quite proud of to this day.

But seeing Janet must've been the dream come true that my mother had always hoped for: A daughter who looked exactly like her. It formed an immediate bond between my mother and her beyond the biological connection. My mom was so excited about their resemblance, which is why I think she felt comfortable telling Janet about the private investigator right away after saying nothing about it to me. For so many years, I'd wished that my mother wouldn't center so much of her attention on me, and now, it looked like my wish was being granted, too. But the outcome was not nearly what I would've expected.

Chapter 18:

Such Devoted Sisters

The first meeting was over, and so began our new life.

Just like the first meeting itself, it wasn't a very dramatic transition to incorporate Janet and her family into the fold of our family dynamic. Our spouses and children all knew of each other, and the interactions between them were quite pleasant. Janet and I would catch up frequently over the phone or at a meal. Phone conversations would happen more often, given the distance between us, but we still got to see each other in person fairly regularly. We did have over 50 years to make up for, after all.

Then, we gradually introduced one another into our respective circles, who had all heard about the reunion between us. I invited Janet to spend a weekend with me and my friends as we were renting a cabin in the mountains. My friends became so excited at the thought of meeting Janet. It was a lovely little weekend getaway that felt as if a group of friends from school were catching up for the first time in several years. She also offered to go out for lunch with my mom and me—I guess I should get used to saying "our mom" now—so we could meet her best friend, who was also great. Everyone got to know everyone very quickly as we all tried to match faces to names while remembering years' worth of memories attached to a given person.

I could hardly contain my excitement. I was already starting to plan upcoming holidays and family get-togethers to see when we could have Janet and her family at my house. I always liked the small group gatherings, but that had become pretty familiar to me. Our family had always been pretty small, so there were almost never more than 10 people around at a given time. It was always quaint and lovely, but after years of the same general experience, I craved a bit of energy. And it felt like we were finally getting that in our own family.

That's not to say I regret having a smaller family when I was young, though. I always loved seeing my relatives, no matter how big the group was. But I do think that upbringing contributed to my fondness for larger gatherings or parties later in life. I was never a party animal, but I liked being amongst a bigger crowd of people, whether it was at prom or my young adult apartment parties. There were more people to meet and talk to, and the eagerness to see other people was higher all around. I thought it was a bit of a thrill to see so many people around me and have the chance to be among all of them.

So, when I realized that I could have a similarly energetic environment in my own family gatherings, it felt like a dream coming true. One thing that brought me the most joy out of everything was that my children finally had their own first cousins. Although my immediate family was quite small, I had quite a few cousins growing up. We spent a ton of time together and made so many great memories. It helped make up for being an only child. I'm still close with them today, which only made me feel worse for my children that they didn't get to experience that same closeness with their own cousins when they were young. But it was better late than never for them to have their own cousins, and I couldn't have been happier for them. It seemed like a promising start.

As for me, I became an aunt for the first time in my life. I always thought it would be fun to be an aunt. They seemed like the person who got to do all the fun parts of parenting with none of the weighty responsibilities. After having taken on that role, I can confirm that it is similar to that. My nieces and nephews were grown up by the time I met them, but it was still fun to be somewhere in between a big sister and a mother to them. Plus, Janet was also a grandmother, so it was fun to be around toddlers too. We hadn't had any young ones in our family for a long time. The adults were great company, but I loved being around the kids, too. They're so soft and adorable.

But far and away the most exciting part of meeting Janet was in strengthening my own relationship with her. I finally got to experience what it was like to have a sister after being an only child for all my life. Ever since my first playdate with Amy, I'd always wanted to know what it was like to have a sister. For all I knew, it was like having a best friend who lived with you and could do anything and everything with you. I thought there would be this inseparable bond that would keep the two of us together forever, and I think I was on the right track in thinking that way.

Don't get me wrong; I absolutely adore all of my dear female friends and cousins; they've been nothing short of remarkable to me. That said, there was something about having a biological sister that always appealed to my younger self greatly. Janet had been filling a 54-year void in my heart that no one else could really address. It was nobody's fault, and I certainly knew that I was loved, but it didn't stop the feelings of loneliness from pressing against my heart from time to time. But with Janet now in my life, I felt like I had a completely unique relationship with her that helped the loneliness fade away. There was someone else who understood the feeling of needing to fend for oneself, which she may have felt even more than I did due to her adoption. It was nice to feel connected to someone in such an intimate way.

On top of that, I found myself starting to imagine what an alternate reality with her in our house would've looked like. In other words, I played the "what if" game with myself—not just in the negative sense of imagining my father's reaction to everything, but in a more positive one. What if I grew up with a big sister? Janet was a few years older than me and definitely portrayed the warmth of one. What if we went up to Auburn as adults and brought our own kids there together? There were times when it would bring me back to being a young mother or even a child again, imagining that this is what could've happened.

Although my imagination would envision several heartwarming moments, I'm also thankful that things worked out in the way they did. I'm sure it wouldn't have been all sunshine and butterflies, either. Since Janet had such an uncanny resemblance to our mother, maybe she would've favored Janet, which would've caused me to resent both of them. Who knows? It's all hypothetical, and the fact of the matter is that Janet came into my life at a wonderful time and grew up to be a wonderful person. I appreciated her so much more after having lived the life that I lived to get to this point.

There were definitely moments sprinkled throughout those early weeks and months of getting to know Janet where it hit me that she didn't grow up with our mother. One that stands out among those memories occurred during Janet's birthday. She was having a party and invited me to join in on the festivities. I was elated to go shopping for her. I finally got to buy a gift for my sister! Every time I went to a store counter and said, "Oh, I'm looking for a birthday present for my sister," I got a little giddy inside. It was nice to be able to say that and have it be real.

I ended up buying Janet a gold necklace that said *Sister* on it (what can I say—ever since a handsome young man gave me some gold jewelry in a car, I've been partial to gold accessories). I couldn't wait to give it to her. I felt so special that I finally had a sister to spoil now, as most of my friends did. The party couldn't come quickly enough. Well, for some, anyway.

While Janet had welcomed my family with open arms, she hadn't told her adoptive mother about the situation. Everything was still fairly new at the time, and it would've been so difficult for Janet to break that news to her adoptive mother. She had been a fabulous mom to Janet and was getting up in years, so Janet didn't think it would be worth it to tell her now. She told me it would've hurt her adoptive mother too much to know that Janet was pursuing these relationships with her biological family.

That scenario added another layer to my lingering question of what the concept of "family" truly meant. I'd always thought about it from my perspective and being the one with the long-lost sister, but it opened my eyes to see more of Janet's side of the story. She had a great family with parents that weren't biologically hers. Were they any less loving? Not at all. Did she still consider them to be her family? Absolutely. But now, there was a qualifier before the term—they weren't just "family," they were the "adoptive family." And Janet didn't want her adoptive mother to have to wrestle with that.

So, when it came time for the party, she told me her decision on what to do.

"You're still more than welcome to come to the party," she said.

"Okay, great, I'd love to come," I responded. "I'll just let our mother know when we should arrive."

"Well, that's the thing," Janet added. "I can see a possibility where you come. I can just tell my adoptive mother that you're a friend, and that's the truth—I see you as a friend just as much as a sister. But I don't think I can invite my biological mom. I can't lie to my mother, and I don't know how I'd introduce my biological mother, especially since I look so much like her. I don't see any other option. I'm so sorry. I feel awful about this."

I could tell that she was being genuine. She had always been so open from the start, so I got the impression that, if she had it her way, everything would be out in the open, and everyone could get along with everyone. But Janet was a dutiful daughter to her adoptive mother, who'd been so good to her for her entire life. It really did seem like a hard decision for her to make, but it was her birthday, and she wanted as little drama to be there as possible, which meant being one person short.

It was also around this time that I noticed my mother's behavior toward me started to change again. Janet and I were spending more time together without her around, and she did not like being left out of things. She had so many questions that all demanded an immediate answer from me.

"So, have you seen Janet recently?" she'd ask.

"Um, I don't know; I saw her on the weekend. Does that count as 'recently'?" I'd respond.

"What'd you do?"

"Just got lunch."

"Who else was there?"

"No one. Just us."

"Okay... You never thought of inviting me?"

"What? I don't... We just wanted sister time, I guess."

"Ha, sister time... It's funny how you didn't even want to meet her before, and now you two can't seem to stop spending time together."

I hated when she did this. She was trying to hint at something without just coming out and saying it. I would actively try to stop myself from rolling my eyes.

"I don't know if I'd call it 'funny,' but it's nice to spend time with her, I'd agree."

"Oh sure, sure. So, when are you seeing her next?"

"Oh, my gosh, I don't know, Mom. Sometime in the near future, probably."

"*Near* future, okay then. When do you think that'll be?"

"I said, I don't know. Are you trying to get at something?"

"No, no. I just find it interesting how my own flesh and blood seem to be so comfortable with each other and without the very person who brought them both into this world."

"Mom, it's not like that. I just have a different relationship with her than I do with you."

"Stop taking everything so personally, Emma. It's just interesting, that's all."

The comments would fluctuate between being passive-aggressive and plain-aggressive. It drove me nuts. But I knew why she was saying them: She was jealous. She saw how much time Janet and I were spending together and how infrequently she would be around during those times. She hated being on the outside of things. She had never been on the outside at any point in her life, and she couldn't stand it. Everyone always fawned over her, but now, neither Janet nor I were showering her with attention. It seemed like our mother wanted Janet all to herself. I think she felt entitled to that outcome and was furious when that wasn't happening.

The thing was it wasn't like we were intentionally trying to exclude our mother. I had my own thoughts on my mom, but I knew it wasn't fair to force Janet to see things my way. That wouldn't have been fair to Janet. She was a grown woman who was more than capable of forming her own opinion. But it's also true that the relationship that one has with a sibling is different than the one they have with a parent, which I learned as I spent more time with Janet. Both types of relationships are important, but they're unique. That time I had a one-on-one with Janet was so valuable in strengthening my ties with her, and that wouldn't have happened if our mother had been there the whole time.

I knew that my mother wanted to be involved, but did she need to be involved in everything? Apparently, she felt that the answer to that was "yes."

It was also at that point that things started to change. I cling to these early memories because the events that followed made things so much more complicated.

Chapter 19:

Safe Travels

Leading up to Janet's party, my mother's mood started altering toward me.

I didn't immediately recognize the transition as it was happening because I had grown used to adversity coming from her. You know by now that my relationship with my mother has been rocky, so seeing her act in an ornery or moody fashion was nothing new. But as the weeks started to pass and I'd been meeting with Janet and her family more regularly, my mother seemed especially annoyed at anything I said or did. Oftentimes, it had nothing to do with Janet herself, but my mother still found a way to be upset with me.

More specifically, it felt like she used any excuse she could to try to pick a fight with me. What started as more passive eye rolls eventually morphed into full-on yelling at me if she was even marginally upset with me. The stupidest little things seemed to completely set her off, whereas in the past, they'd just mildly annoy her. Everything was made out to be this huge deal when they were often minor inconveniences at worst.

For example, on one particular day, she brought up something very out of the blue and in a demanding tone.

"Emma, where's my passport?" she asked.

I was taken aback by the question. It had been in the same place for several years, so I didn't know why she was asking about it. "Uh, upstairs in our safe. Why?"

"I want it back."

"Okay, yeah, sure. Are you going somewhere?"

"No. I just think it would be a good idea to have it in my house in case I need it for anything."

"Okay… I mean, it's your passport, you can do what you want with it, but it's no trouble for us if you want to leave it in the safe. It's secure in there."

Her eyes rolled. "Why do you insist on making everything more difficult?! Just give me my damn passport and stop being such a brat."

I sighed. It was no use fighting that. "Alright, okay, I'll go get it."

I went upstairs to grab her passport from our safe and handed it back to her, which she promptly swiped from my hand. She tucked it into her purse and zipped it back up to make sure that nobody took it from her, I guess. I don't know why anyone in my house would want her passport.

It all felt very shifty. We had stored my mother's passport for years because we actually had a safe to make sure that nothing happened to it. My mother had never had any issues leaving her passport with us. If anything, it was one less thing for her to have to worry about; she didn't have to remember where she stored such an important piece of ID in her own house, and it wasn't like she'd be using it regularly anyway. Why would she suddenly want it back now, as a senior citizen with no intention of traveling anywhere?

What made it even more bizarre was that she rarely traveled without us. Even when she was a few years younger, she almost never did long trips or solo trips, certainly none that required a passport. She was doing fine living on her own, but we wouldn't want her to do any major traveling by herself. I couldn't wrap my head around why she insisted on having it now, but I also didn't want to go through another round of scolding.

By this point in my life, I was sick of going through the same routine with her. Typically, I'm not someone who likes to stir up arguments, but I'm also not afraid to push back if I don't think something is right. But with my mother, it felt like it took years of experience to make so little progress. As a child, I just did what she wanted to have done; as an adult, I gradually tried pushing back but always ended up caving to whatever she wanted to have happen. I hated it. She constantly made me feel like our conversations were competitions I was bound to lose. She always had to be right while making me feel stupid for believing anything else.

The passport story is just one example of many I could pull from, but things generally followed that routine with her for a while. She'd ask for something, I'd question it, she'd get irrationally angry about it, I'd settle for her request, and she'd passive-aggressively grunt and pout as her way of cooling off. It was irritating, to say the least, but manageable. I thought I knew how to handle or, at least, what to expect of her emotional spats after a lifetime of dealing with them.

However, there was one incident that changed my perception of that belief.

It happened on a Sunday evening around 9:00. My mother was spending the night at our house, which she would often do. The two of us were sitting at the kitchen table, with my mother watching *Gilligan's Island* reruns as I was quietly working away on my laptop. All in all, it was a pretty casual night.

Meanwhile, James had been in the family room for quite some time. Once the evening had rolled around, I honestly forgot that he was down there. He made his way up the stairs, but he was barefoot, so neither my mother nor I heard him come up. He was also carrying a pair of shoes at the time, noticing that my mom and I were in our respective zones. He thought of a creative way to get our attention.

BANG!

He slammed the soles of his shoes together as hard as he could to make the loudest sound possible.

After hearing the bang, I jumped in my seat. I whipped my head around to see what had happened, but once I saw James holding his shoes, I smiled, put my hand on my chest, and laughed it off with a sigh of relief. Classic James. He wasn't a huge jokester, but he'd do the occasional light-hearted prank from time to time. It was all in good fun, and it kept me on my toes.

That's a natural reaction to have, I think. But based on my mother's reaction, you would've thought my husband had tried to murder her. She aggressively stood up, pushing her chair a few feet backward to glare at my husband.

"What the hell is your problem?!" she screamed. "You just gave me a heart attack! Are you trying to kill me?"

My husband and I started chuckling a bit more as my heart rate slowed down to a normal speed. We knew it was harmless and thought my mother was just playing up the situation. She really captured the shock of being startled by someone when she was least expecting it.

"I guess you're awake now, huh?" James teased.

"That's not funny!" My mother kept screaming. "How could you do something like that?!"

"Ah, you know it's just for fun, Doris," he said. "Don't worry; I'm all done for the night. No more pranks, I promise. I'm gonna head up to bed; I'll see you ladies tomorrow. Good night, everybody."

With that, he made his way up the stairs. I watched him make his way up there and thought it might be a good time to retire myself.

"You know, Mom," I started, staring at the staircase, "I think I might head up soon, too. I'm feeling—"

"There is *no* way I'm sleeping after that!" she yelled.

Now, I'd jumped in place a second time as my mother's raised voice jolted my attention toward her. She began frantically walking around the room and kept screaming at the top of her lungs.

"That was one of the rudest things I've ever seen! I have *never* seen such disrespect in my entire life! Not once! That... that *maniac* of a man thinks he can just stroll in here and do something like that?!"

"Okay, Mom, it's fine. It's over now. You can stop with the act."

"Shut up! It is *not* an act; how dare you even say that!"

My mother kept walking around in circles in our kitchen, screaming all kinds of profanities and inappropriate names directed toward my husband. I don't feel the need to mention all of them here, but I will include some of the words she used in this chapter (and beyond) so that you get a sense of the tone of this conversation. I'm sure you'll get the point, even in my abridged version. Her rant was vulgar and nasty to listen to, but that wasn't the end of it.

My mother was hysterical. She would not calm down and made it known throughout the house (and most likely the whole neighborhood). Of course, it's impossible to sleep when there's someone having an absolute meltdown in your kitchen. After several minutes, James marched his way down the stairs to confront my mother's crazy antics. He'd had enough.

"Doris, do you have any sense of how loud you're being right now?" He asked. "Do you know how rude it is to scream bloody murder at night when you're in somebody else's house? I've been trying to sleep and can't even come close because of your relentless yelling."

"You are in NO place to lecture me, asshole!" my mother retorted.

"Mom! That's enough!" I shot back at her in defense of my husband. "Don't you ever call him that!"

"Whoa, okay, that's a bit much," James said. "Fine, I'm sorry. I made a joke that clearly didn't land right. I won't do it again. Are we good now?"

"No, we are not good, you bastard!" my mother roared back at him.

"Excuse me?" James marched right up to her. "I don't care who you are, but you do *not* talk to me like that when you're in *my* house. It doesn't matter that you're my wife's mother; I will NOT stand for any of that!"

"Listen here, you little shit. I will talk however I want, whenever I want."

"Not while you're under my roof, you won't!" he shouted.

"Both of you, please stop!" I wailed. I had been caught standing between the two of them, screaming at the top of my lungs for them to lay off, but neither one would back down. Unfortunately, my voice got drowned out by both of theirs. I was trapped in No Man's Land, waiting for both sides to stop firing at each other, but the fighting seemed to go on forever. Looking back, that was probably the only thing that prevented at least one of them from getting physical with one another, so maybe it was good for something.

In the 30 years that my husband and I had been together by this point, nothing like this had ever happened between him and my mother. I can still picture how loud and vile those remarks were between the two of them. James and my mother kept firing back and forth with each other, waiting to see who would have the final blow to end it all.

I think part of the reason why this turned into such a heated exchange was that, for a brief moment, when those shoe bottoms made contact, my mother felt lost. I think she felt threatened that my husband had somehow bested her at something by catching her off guard—which, again, meant a loss of control for her. She had to know what everyone was doing at all times and had to be the one to come out on top of any situation.

But in the past, when he had done something she didn't expect, she'd freak out for a minute or two before calming down. This time, though, she wasn't calming down. She was getting more heated with every word that came out of her mouth. It was following the pattern she had been establishing of getting disproportionately angry about something inconsequential in the grand scheme of things. Now, she was all in for the fight, and she was determined to win.

My husband was shocked that she'd taken this incident so seriously; it wasn't like he was showing her a new side of himself that she had never seen before. But he knew better than almost anyone how badly my mother had wounded me over the years. He also knew how much pain she'd caused my father, who meant a lot to me and had always been kind to James. I think he wanted to put an end to everything once and for all. So, he uttered the words that he intended to be the nail in the coffin of this argument.

"Doris, if you don't stop this ridiculous, inappropriate behavior, then you'd better get the hell out of my house!"

My mother scoffed. "You can't tell me what to do."

"I just did."

He laid down his trump card. My mom stared him down for a moment, sending daggers into his eyes before delivering her final line.

"Fine. I hate you and hope you die."

She brushed past me and James as she went to grab her things. I couldn't believe this was all happening.

"No, wait, Mom, don't go," I called after her, frantically trying to keep up with her as she gathered her belongings.

"Don't you dare follow me," she scowled. "I'm getting the hell out of this house. Your husband told me to leave, so I'm leaving."

"Well, it's *my* house, too, and it's also 9:00 at night. You have 120 miles to drive, and I don't want you doing that when it's dark outside."

"I said I'm going!"

I kept scampering behind her like a duckling, trying desperately to convince my mother to stay.

"Mom, please!"

"Oh, piss off, will ya?"

"Just stay; we can work this out tomorrow!"

"Shut up! Shut the hell up! You and your rotten husband."

She kept rummaging through her things and shoving them into whatever bag she'd brought with her. Finally, she made her way to the front door with all of her things. It was her last chance to change her mind.

"Mom, stop. You don't have to do this. Just stay. Please."

She looked me square in the eyes.

"I'm going home."

She slammed the door behind her as she left.

Chapter 20:

Excuses and Executors

I had to go for a walk.

My body was too tense to stand still. I had to get out of that house. The air felt stuffy, and I couldn't look around at those walls without thinking of my mother and husband yelling at each other. Walking never failed to help me clear my head and come to my senses.

Once I stepped outside and had a moment to breathe, I called my mom's cell phone. I knew she was driving, which already made me nervous, but I had to talk to her and get to the bottom of what just happened.

Please pick up, I begged to myself. *Please, Mom. Please, please…*

Ring…

Ri—

"What?"

"Mom, please come back."

"No."

"Will you just—"

"Emma, I swear, I will hang up this phone right now if you ask me that again."

"Okay, fine, then, can you just tell me how you're doing? I don't like the idea of you driving in the dark for two hours by yourself. Please talk to me."

"You wanna know how I'm doing? I'm pissed off; that's how I'm doing! Your husband has some nerve talking to me that way."

"I agree that it got out of control there, but that was never his intention."

"Well, clearly, he had some bad intentions. He wouldn't have banged those damn shoes together if it was all pure and good."

"He was just making a joke, Mom. He didn't mean anything by it."

"Don't speak for him. He knows what he did."

"Well, I've lived with him for over 30 years, so I'd like to think that I know a thing or two about him as well."

"Oh, so you *are* taking his side, then? So what, are you just calling me to rub the whole thing in my face?"

"No! I just—I don't know! Look, I don't want you two fighting. I'm sure we can work this out in some way. You're not too far out of town yet; can't you just turn around and come back?"

"Emma, let me make this clear to you: I will never speak to your husband or step foot in your house again."

I thought she was kidding.

I didn't dare test that assumption, though. Instead, I talked to her for the whole two hours until she got back to her house. Part of it was to ease my conscience of knowing she arrived safely; between night driving and her heightened emotions, I didn't want her to make any reckless driving decisions. I was thankful to know that she didn't intentionally or unintentionally crash into something or stop by a bar on the way home. This night didn't need to end in total tragedy.

The other part of my decision to stay on the phone with her was to try to talk her down from that blow-up with the faintest bit of hope that it would persuade her to come back to my house. I think it ended up being more beneficial for me than it did for her. Clearly, my mother wasn't coming back that night, but it gave both of us some space to blow off our emotional steam. I'd tried to do that in the middle of the argument between her and James, but my feeble attempts at raising my voice went nowhere and were listened to by no one. I still wasn't convinced that my mother was listening to me properly on the other end of the phone, but at least it was still a chance for me to get my thoughts out.

When my mother pulled into her driveway, we ended the conversation pretty abruptly.

"I'm home now, Emma."

"Okay, good. Thanks for letting me know you got back safely—"

"Bye."

Call ended.

Okay, well, that could've been worse, I thought to myself. *She isn't dead, and she is still willing to talk to me... somewhat willing, at least. That's something. Her reactions are a bit drastic, but that's not unusual for her. I hope this thing with James will blow over, and we can just move on from everything. It won't happen tomorrow, but hopefully, it won't take too long for her to change her mind.*

I was right in thinking that it wouldn't happen the next day.

I was wrong in thinking it wouldn't take her too much longer.

She never did change her mind. Over the next couple of months, I did my best to stay neutral, especially when I was with my mother. I did not take sides. I avoided as many potential topics of contention as possible. I didn't want anyone in my family to use that as fodder to try to rehash the same argument over again.

It's exhausting to play the role of the middle person in an argument. While you could make the case that it's not as volatile as firmly planting your allegiance to one side, it's still difficult to try to manage the emotions of both sides. And in situations where you agree with one of the sides but can't betray the other one, it just makes it more complicated to know how to act. The middle role is just left to absorb all of the weight of both parties and try to make nice with everyone without having too much of a say themselves.

I didn't like being in that position, but I wanted to keep up as normal a relationship with my family members as possible. Of course, James and I were on the same team, so that was no problem. But things were even relatively stable with my mother and me, which was a pleasant surprise to witness. I would go out of my way to visit her and take her to doctor's appointments, and I made it a point to celebrate her birthday with her.

As far as I knew, everything was okay between me and my mom. She even told me not to tell Janet about the fight she had with my husband. I was surprised she wanted to keep that knowledge between us, but it was also a triggering subject, so I respected her wishes.

Then, after a few months, I got a phone call out of the blue from my Aunt May, who's my mother's sister. I was relieved to see her name, figuring that talking to her would mean that I'd have a break from the drama. I eagerly answered her call and looked forward to hearing how she was doing.

"Hi, Aunt May!" I said. "How are you?"

"Hi, hon. Well, I gotta tell you… I don't really know how to answer that." Her voice trembled on the other end of the phone. It sounded like she was on the verge of crying.

"Hey, what's going on?" I asked with more concern. "Are you okay?"

"Oh yeah, I'm not sick or anything like that, but…" she breathed heavily into the phone. "I haven't been able to sleep all week. I just have this awful news, and I promised I wouldn't say anything about it, but… Oh, I just couldn't live with myself if I didn't tell you what was really going on."

I froze. I didn't know what to make of that comment. My aunt had never sounded so distressed before.

For context, my Aunt May is one of the sweetest people in the world and an excellent person to confide in. If someone were to tell her a secret, regardless of how big it might've been, she would never repeat it to anyone. She's as trustworthy, loyal, and honest a person as there is. So, when she said that she had to tell me a secret, I knew it was a big deal.

"I'm sorry, I—I don't understand," I fumbled over my words.

"It's not your fault at all, which is what makes this so much harder," my aunt continued. "You've always been so good to my sister, and you don't deserve to be treated this way."

What now? I thought to myself. *She was never this nervous when it came to me having a sister, which I only found out about five months ago. Could anything possibly top that?*

It could.

My throat instantly became parched. I tried to swallow as hard as I could before trying to soothe my aunt. I was nervous out of my mind, but I recognized that I had to be the calmer one of the two of us if this conversation was going to go anywhere.

"Okay, well, don't worry, I'm here," I said. "I'll be listening whenever you're ready to speak. Take as much time as you need."

I didn't want to put pressure on her because this was so out of character for her to be doing this, but I was dying to know what she had to say. Thankfully, she didn't keep me in suspense for too long.

"Okay," my aunt began. "Two weeks ago... Your mother and Janet went to a lawyer. Behind your back. They took you out of your mother's will completely... and replaced you with Janet."

My heart sank.

"Janet's the executor of her will now."

My eyes welled up.

I had no words.

"She told me about it last week," Aunt May continued, "and wanted to make sure that you never found out about it. At least, not while she was still alive. She wanted you to have to wait to hear about it after she died so that the three of you could just keep acting as if nothing had changed."

I couldn't believe what I was hearing. I had to grip my chest just to make sure I wasn't hyperventilating in place.

"Why?" was all that my breathy voice could muster.

"I don't know. Because she's a cruel, cruel woman," my aunt went on. "I guess it was her way of not having to deal with the situation and feeling like she could have the last laugh. I can never understand how someone could think that way about anyone, never mind their own daughter."

I couldn't hold back my tears as I watched them fall onto the floor. It brought me back to sitting in my Enfield bathroom while my mom brushed my hair. In those days, she was only ripping out my hair. Now, she was ripping out my heart.

"But, if you want a fuller answer to that question," my aunt added, "my sister justified it by saying that it had to do with your husband banging his shoes together that one night. She said that it scared her so much that she didn't want him to reap any benefits from her. Therefore, she couldn't leave you with anything because that would mean that he'd get whatever you got."

Bingo.

That was the excuse she was looking for. She had to find a reason to cut me out of her life permanently, and the shoe-slamming incident seemed to be the closest thing she could find to one. She certainly jumped at that chance when it came up.

Then, it dawned on me that she had been setting this up for a while, looking for her opportunities to cut ties with me. Changing her attitude toward me, asking for her passport back... she was trying to distance herself from me, and picking a fight with my husband was the finishing touch.

I couldn't grasp all the thoughts that were racing through my mind. How could my mother and Janet both sneak around and betray me like this? She couldn't have a face-to-face conversation with me to talk things out before even considering replacing me with Janet?

For my entire adult life, I had always been listed as her executor, and all of that was stripped away in a matter of moments. I felt the same way about it as I did about her life insurance policy when she made Dale the beneficiary (I wonder if she ever replaced Dale with Janet or if I was the only one who got written out)—I didn't want her money, but I thought I was at least worthy of her trust. Despite our differences, I'd done my best to have a civil relationship with my mother, but she just kept finding ways to write me out of her life. And now that my mother had been telling my aunt these things and insisting that she keep it a secret from me, it felt like she wanted to ostracize me from my own family.

Then, I remembered Dad's ashes.

The executor of my mother's will would be able to decide what would happen to them. I'd been holding out hope for years that whenever my mom went, I could have Dad brought back into my home for good. But now that I wasn't the executor, I'd probably never see them again. Janet wouldn't have any use for them, and if she was already close enough with my mother to have her be the new executor, I doubted she'd let me have them.

176

I realized that it wasn't just my mother's life that I wouldn't be able to preserve by not being her executor. It would affect how much I could keep from my dad's life, too.

That's what infuriated me.

How could someone decide to make another person the executor of their will only five months after meeting them? I know Janet was my mother's biological daughter, but she didn't know anything else about her for 56 years. For all my mother knew, Janet was a stranger who looked strikingly similar to her. Five months is not enough time to determine whether someone is fit to play such a massive role in handling someone's estate. I don't care what anybody says.

But not only did my mother assign this role to someone she barely knew, but she did so at the expense of the only child she actually raised and knew about for over half a century. Does that suddenly not matter because of a minor prank? Of course not. It has always sounded more than a little fishy to me and everyone else who has heard this story. There's no way that anyone, even my mother, could make such a big leap from such a small gesture.

Albert Einstein once said, "The more I learn, the more I realize how much I don't know" (in Goodreads, 2020, para. 1), and that couldn't be truer. It felt like every new piece of information I learned about my mother only made me feel more alienated from her. I thought I knew her pretty well, but as these secrets kept on revealing themselves, I realized that I really didn't know all that much. At this point, I wondered if I knew Janet better than her, although I realized that I really didn't know her at all.

Well, if I had anything to say about it, that was going to change. I was going to confront the two of them and find out exactly what was going on, starting with Janet.

Chapter 21:

Message Received

After exchanging a few more words, I hung up the phone with my aunt.

That poor woman. She would've had her own collection of experiences growing up dealing with my mother as a sister. Aunt May didn't just know my mom as a person, but she truly understood what it was like to live with her. Because of that, she was one of the few people with whom I could talk about my mother, in all honesty. My aunt's loyalty to me never wavered despite whatever turmoil I was going through with my mother, and Aunt May and I always maintained a strong relationship as a result.

It's funny how siblings can turn out to be such different people despite their genetic and, in the case of my mom and aunt, environmental similarities. I know that things like birth order and personal experiences could affect the level of responsibility versus rebellion that each child takes on, but there are almost always still shared qualities between siblings. Yet, my mother quickly garnered a reputation for fibbing her way through life, while my aunt could never tell a lie. Same parents, same house, but almost opposite personalities. Just interesting, that's all.

At any rate, Aunt May did her best to tell me the truth and did so valiantly. I'll forever be grateful to her for recognizing what was right and letting me know what was going on. Bless her beautiful heart.

Without taking too much time in between calls, I scrolled down to Janet's contact information. I wanted to ride off of the adrenaline that had been rushing through my body without overthinking things too much. Those are the times when I'm more likely to cave to other people's preferences. No, this time, I didn't want anything to stop me from getting to the truth.

I tapped Janet's name and began the call.

Ring…

Ring…

Ring…

Ri—

"Hello?"

"Hi, Janet. It's Emma."

"Oh, hey, Emma, how are you? I bet you have questions about my party. I can't wait. I'm so excited that you'll be there!"

If only she knew.

"Well, um, I've been better, but I actually wanted to talk to you about something else that I just heard."

"Oh, okay, yeah, for sure. Let's chat."

I heard some shuffling around, which told me that Janet was probably sitting down. Wise move.

"What's going on?" she said.

"Basically… I heard that you're now the executor of my mom's will. Is that true?"

Silence.

"And that you went to a lawyer with my mom to have my name removed and your name added on instead."

More silence.

I thought she'd hung up the phone.

"Hello?"

Nothing.

"Janet?"

"You need to ask your mother about that."

Hmm. Well, that was an interesting response.

"Okay, I can do that. Bye, Janet."

"Bye."

Call ended.

I knew that I was going to catch her off guard, but I didn't expect the response to be so uncommunicative. I mean, her silence spoke volumes, but the fact that she didn't have anything to say to me after I brought it up wasn't a promising start. I already knew that my aunt's word was solid, but now I definitely had cause for concern.

Immediately after finishing the brief interaction with Janet, I scrolled to my mom's contact information. Time for round two.

Ring…

Ring…

Ri—

"Hello?"

"Hi, Mom. Can I talk to you about something?" I was honestly past the point of pleasantries. I didn't need to ask how my mom was doing. I was fed up with the charade and wanted to get to the bottom of it. Plus, if anyone in my family could appreciate directness and brevity, it would be my mother.

"Umm… yeah, okay," she said.

"Did you take Janet to the lawyer's office to make her the executor of your will?"

She paused briefly, but it was nowhere near as long as Janet's pause.

"No."

"I know you're lying to me, Mom."

"I'm not lying to you. How dare you accuse me of lying to you?"

"Don't pull that with me. It's not the first time you've done this, and it won't be the last. I'm gonna ask you again: Did you go with Janet to the lawyer's office and have my name removed from your will?"

"And I'm gonna give you the same answer again: No!"

She was adamant; I'll give her that. I knew it would be more work to get it out of her. Not too surprising.

"Mom, I'm not just making this stuff up. I know you've told people about this."

"Well, then, who told you? Who is your so-called source?"

"I'd rather not say." Aunt May had risked her relationship with my mother to tell me this information, so I didn't want to reveal her name unless I absolutely had to.

"See? You can't even tell me who told you this information—false information, at that. It's not true."

"That doesn't make it untrue; that just means that *I* actually understand a thing or two about loyalty."

"Which I have shown you all your life. I'm the best damn mother you could've ever asked for. I would put food on the table for you; I would pick you up from school, I would—"

"No, you wouldn't! I walked to school both ways every single day! And stop changing the subject. See, it's exactly this kind of thing that makes me totally believe that you replaced me with Janet."

"Emma, that's enough."

"No, it's not. I know that the two of you went behind my back because you wanted to pretend that everything was normal between the three of us until you died. That way, I'd have to discover your betrayal in the moment because you didn't want to have to deal with me in person. Great job, Mom. You wanted to be a coward instead of a mother."

I'll admit, I was a bit surprised at myself. I'd spent far too many years shrinking back at my mother's demands, but this time, I was able to be bold. It felt good. Really, really good.

But it wasn't over yet.

"Are you finished?" My mother tried to sound bored or disinterested, but I knew I was getting under her skin.

"Not even close. You were looking for your way out for the longest time, trying to find a way to get rid of me once and for all. You looked for your openings, trying to pick fights with me whenever you could. You even took your passport back before anything major happened between us so that you wouldn't have to depend on me or my family for anything. And then, it hit you—my family and, more specifically, my husband. If you couldn't find something wrong with me, then you could certainly find something wrong with him. And BANG! The shoe incident. You acted so wildly immature in that moment because you wanted to make it out to be some big, traumatic event that would justify your decision to write me out of your will. Well, guess what? It wasn't. Not even close. It was a freaking joke. But you made it seem like he'd tried to kill you when that was nowhere near his intention. But it didn't matter because now you could use that event as leverage. So, I'll bet you called Janet shortly after that incident, and gave her a generic enough rundown to make it look like you were the victim in the situation—which wasn't true—so that she would agree to become the new executor of your will. That's why you didn't want me to talk to her about the shoe-slamming fiasco because if I'd explained what actually happened to her, she would've seen that *you* were the instigator, not James! But by making my husband out to be the problem, it would be easier for her to get on board with your offer and ensure that I wouldn't see one iota of your belongings. So, you two met with the lawyer, got everything signed that needed signing, and made nice with me to pretend like everything was cool between us. And you told people in secret not to say anything to me so that the knife would dig even deeper into my back when I eventually found out. That way, it would make me look like the idiot who didn't know any better while you could supposedly rest in peace. Is that not true?"

I had to catch my breath after that one.

I was in a state of shock after my rant. I couldn't believe that I'd finally gotten everything off of my chest. Although I only found out about the will a few minutes before calling my mother, some of these thoughts had been ruminating for weeks. Well, the sentiments had lasted for decades, but ever since the huge fight in my house, I'd been wanting to tell her exactly how it made me feel. It was my chance, and I took it as best as I could.

Once I had a second to stabilize myself, I realized that my mother hadn't said anything yet. I'd come too far to settle for less than the truth—the transparent, direct, and honest-to-goodness truth.

"Is that not true?" I repeated myself.

Her answer to this question would change the status of our relationship forever. She'd either be a lying coward or a lying backstabber. How she chose to proceed was up to her.

I heard a faint exhale on the other end.

"It's true."

Lying backstabber.

It finally happened. My mother had finally conceded to something, maybe for the first time in her life. And I was going to let her have it.

"I knew it. I freaking knew it! You lied to me! To my face *and* behind my back. You knew how badly this would hurt me, and you did it anyway! What kind of sick, twisted person writes their own child out of their will and hands over the executorship to some person she's only met after five months?!"

"HEY!"

It was the first time my mother had raised her voice over the entire conversation.

"Don't you dare talk about Janet in that way! You know damn well that she's your sister just as much as she is my daughter."

"To hell with that! No sister of mine would betray me like this and agree to take away the one tiny access I would have to MY FUCKING FAMILY! Because, oh yeah, half of the estate that she would be in charge of handling belongs to *my* father! Not *her* father, MY father—a father I actually knew and loved!"

Did I cross a line there? Maybe. But I couldn't deny how I felt and had thrown my filter out the window.

"Watch your mouth," my mother demanded of me.

"No! I'm sick of your bullshit! He was *my* father! And she—"

It was getting hard to breathe amidst all the crying and hyperventilating, but I tried my best to get it all out there.

"And she's gonna have the right to handle *all* of his stuff! His ashes, Mom. His ashes! They're gonna be hers. You *knew* I wanted those years ago, and you did jackshit about it. Because that's the kind of shit you tried to pull for my entire life, you fucking bitch!"

I could go on, but I'm sure you understand the gist of it. The rest of the conversation did not go well. There was a lot of yelling, cursing, and crying, mostly on my part. I was an unhinged wreck.

My voice started to croak because my throat had become strained from screaming. I couldn't use a solid tone of voice anymore, but I did my darndest to fight through it. I'm surprised I still have functioning vocal cords today.

This went on for several minutes until James came into the dining room where I had been sitting. I'd almost forgotten that I wasn't home alone because I was so absorbed in what was happening on the other end of the phone. The look in James' eye was one of both concern and horror.

"Good grief, woman," he said to me. "Hang up that damn phone before you have a stroke."

He had a point.

I'd gotten all of the important things off of my chest, and if I were to continue any longer, I would've put myself in an early grave. My executors certainly know who they are.

After a few shallow breaths, I angled my phone so the microphone was aimed directly at my mouth.

"I hope you two enjoy your lives together!" I screeched.

With that, I pushed my finger on the red circle as hard as I possibly could.

That was when everything began to dawn on me. I dropped my phone onto the table. I couldn't stop shaking. I buried my head into my hands as James pulled up a chair and held me silently. I sobbed uncontrollably.

For so many years of my life, I felt like I had a mother but no sister. Then, it felt like I had a narcissistic mother and, for a few months, a wonderful sister. Now, it felt like I had no mother or sister at all. I was truly an orphan now.

I couldn't wrap my head around the situation. All the sneaking around behind my back between my mother and Janet, all the while acting like they were best friends with me to my face. I started to question the authenticity of my relationships with both of them. Was any of it real? Did my mom fake everything to pass the time until she could get in touch with Janet? Did Janet just make nice with me as a way to learn more about my mom? I didn't know what to think, but I wasn't prepared to think of anything good.

Everyone who knows this story generally says the same thing: "Well, Janet should never have accepted those terms! She should've said that she didn't want to be involved in that because it would've caused a problem between you two." And I agree. I would've said the same thing to them if the tables were turned and I was hearing their story.

But while it's nice to have their reassurance now, I still felt like the odd woman out in my own family when this was all happening. My mother and Janet seemed to be on the same page about everything, while I seemed like the crazy one for wanting to have an honest relationship with my mother and sister. It was so backward.

I was totally ready and even excited to embrace Janet into my life. I bought her a gold necklace that said "sister," for goodness' sake. Those have extra significance to me, and I was willing to extend that special meaning to include her, but that was completely betrayed. I couldn't fathom the idea of someone agreeing to those terms while this was happening, and I still can't fathom it now. I guess we all have different priorities.

Did I even want a sister in my life if this was the kind of thing she was willing to do to me? I didn't think so. As far as I knew, neither Janet nor my mother were people I felt that I could ever trust again.

Needless to say, I never ended up making it to Janet's party. After learning about this news, I couldn't bring myself to be in the same room as her. I ended up returning the necklace, which was really disappointing. My first present for a sibling ended up exactly where I had found it as if I never had a sister to give it to in the first place.

Chapter 22:

Learning How to Stand Tall

The following week was the worst week of my life.

That's not a statement I make lightly. I'm not the type of person who complains about everything wrong with the world or allows things to get me down. I believe we're bound to experience things that challenge us in many different ways. While we might have some control over our situations, there are also a lot of times when things happen that are beyond our control. In either case, I think we should focus primarily on our reaction to our circumstances rather than the event itself. What's done is done, but we can still have some say over what we say and do about it.

Because of that mentality, I've been a pretty determined person for most of my life. I'm usually able to shake things off and move on; sometimes, it happens more quickly than at other times, but it almost always arrives at the same resolution.

Not this time, though.

I'd never had anything of this magnitude happen to me before, and I was completely dysfunctional. I couldn't work. I couldn't sleep. I couldn't eat. It felt like I was walking around with my mind in a constant fog. Every day was the same shade of gray. I couldn't bring myself to find any kind of enjoyment in my life because this massive betrayal was weighing me down. My mother had always been my Achilles' heel, but this felt like she'd taken a sledgehammer to both feet and caused me to come crumbling to the ground.

I couldn't think about anything else. It was the first thing I thought about when I woke up in the morning and the last thing I thought about when I went to bed at night. I kept replaying my sister's and my mother's words over the phone as they either shifted the blame, denied the incident, or tried to make me feel bad for questioning them. I couldn't stop revisiting their behavior over the last few months in my head as they tried to pretend that everything was okay. Meanwhile, my mother was using all those niceties to gaslight me into thinking that there was nothing else going on.

And, perhaps worst of all, I couldn't help but imagine what happened during the events that I wasn't around to witness. How did my mom initiate the topic of conversation with Janet? What was Janet's response? What was the general mood in the car as they drove to the lawyer's office? What did the lawyer say about everything? Were they eager to get things done? Did it satisfy my mother to see my name being deleted from her will?

I was utterly exhausted by the preoccupation of all these thoughts. I was riddled with questions that I didn't want to have answered, although they'd continue to torture me if they were left unaddressed. My eyes drooped for days on end. No amount of makeup or skincare product could conceal those dark circles. I don't think I held my head up straight for that entire week. It would sink anytime I didn't have to lift it to see where I was going.

Yet, on top of these perpetual feelings of numbness, my week would be punctuated with extreme emotional outbursts and jabs of pain. I was crying all the time. My heart felt like a knife had been stabbed through it, and I couldn't wiggle it out. I constantly felt sick to my stomach, which repulsed me from any kind of nourishment. It felt like my body was rejecting any glimmer of hope because it just could not see another way out.

My family did their best to support me during this time, but they also knew I wasn't in a place to be consoled. James was wonderful. He did a lot of the heavy lifting in terms of taking care of the house that week because I was just not in a place to do that. I probably would've been a greater hazard to myself or them if I had been entrusted with too much responsibility. I thank God that James let me mourn over these events as much as I needed to while he was equipped to take over some of those tasks temporarily.

It was through my close relationships with people like James, Amy, and Carin that I had a healthy view of relationships, romantic or otherwise. I have rarely had an intimate connection with someone where the workload and emotional burden of the relationship was evenly split all the time. There would be times when I would carry a bit more of the weight or help out more with certain tasks, and there would be times when the other person would do more of that work for me. Because there was a strong foundation of love and respect in that relationship, we'd understand that there would be times when each person would play certain roles. Sometimes, that meant helping out more, and at other times, that meant being helped out more. We'd recognize one another's strengths and the various circumstances happening in our lives that would affect how to proceed.

But when it came to my relationship with my mother, there was never an understanding of that mutual give and take; it was a one-sided dynamic where I gave, and she took. She felt entitled to get as much as she could from our relationship while putting forth as little effort as necessary to hold onto it. Any effort she did put forward was conditional in that she had to be in the mood to help out and would expect that it would still benefit her in some way. Most of that centered around my children. She'd go to considerable lengths to make them happy because she liked having grandchildren around. But when it came to me, she only saw me as valuable when she wanted something that only I could provide. Once Janet came along, though, it didn't take her long to replace me.

Despite being a mentally strong person, my mother was the one person who could disarm me. I even took the time to learn about her various tactics, but my preparation could only get me so far. She always ended up getting her way. As I got older, I learned how to fight back a little bit, but it kind of felt like firing an arrow into a brick wall. Sure, a bow and arrow is still a weapon, but it doesn't really have much of an impact against that fortress. Yet, the warrior in me still felt like there could be a chance that I'd penetrate the barrier in some way. For a long time, I thought that meant finding a tiny crevice in the wall's foundation that would allow my arrow to sneak through and possibly reach her on the other side. At this point, though, a part of me just wanted a ceasefire.

After that horrible week was over, I started to wonder to myself, *Would my mother or Janet ever want to reach out to me? Maybe enough time has passed that they'd like to reconnect. I don't know if I'm ready for that, but it would be nice to hear from them.*

That's when I started to anticipate that either my mother or Janet might call at any time. I waited to hear from them at all hours of the day. I'd jump at the sound of my phone ringing and desperately looked at the caller ID to see who it was.

Unknown number.

Amy.

Unknown number.

Wrong number.

James.

Amy.

Unknown number.

Carin.

Unknown number.

Unknown number.

Every time, I got my hopes up, and every time, I was let down.

I started paying closer attention to our mail deliveries. *Maybe they'd write me a letter instead,* I thought. *They wouldn't have to hear my voice that way, and they already know where I live. It makes sense.*

So, I turned my attention toward our deliveries. I'd sort through the mail as quickly as I could once it was dropped off.

Flyers.

Phone bill.

TV bill.

Flyers.

More flyers.

Internet bill.

Okay, I thought, *maybe they won't send anything out of the blue. Maybe they'd wait until a major holiday rolled around and use that as an excuse to reconnect.*

My birthday passed.

Holiday after holiday passed.

I never heard a word.

A year had gone by in this manner before I finally gave up hope of hearing from Janet or my mother. It was too mentally exhausting to continue getting my hopes up and being disappointed every time. My heart had been through too much pain for me to expose it to even more of it willingly. I was done.

I realized that I would find far greater contentment in releasing the situation than trying to cling to something desperately that wasn't there. My mother and Janet had chosen to walk away from a life with me in it, yet I was trying to tell myself that it was salvageable. I knew that a change in mindset wouldn't necessarily change the fact that it could still be restored, but I had to let that happen organically. I couldn't imprison my thoughts on this idea that they would reach out to me. I still had to keep living my life, with or without my mother or sister's involvement. And if they were going to continue acting in this way, then I realized that it would actually be easier to move forward without them.

That doesn't mean that it was an easy decision, though. They were still my family, and I so badly wanted to hope we'd be together again. But I saw how this issue had been controlling my life for a year to the detriment of my well-being and that of my husband and children. I couldn't let them live with me in this state, nor did I want to remain in this state. So, that meant that something had to go. I had the choice of releasing my mother and sister or my husband and children. It wasn't a choice, really. I had to let my mother and sister go. But I was finally in a place where I was ready to let that happen.

It felt very freeing. I could focus more of my time and energy on people who truly loved me and valued my presence. I no longer carried this massive weight on my shoulders to feel like I had to be at my mother's or sister's beck and call whenever they were ready to repair the relationship. I knew that I hadn't done anything wrong, but during that time, I still felt like I had to prove something to them, like I was still a loyal daughter and sister. While it may have started from a good place, I needed time to remember the mutuality of relationships, as I discussed earlier in the chapter. I couldn't force myself to be close to people who didn't want to be close to me. I shouldn't have to convince anybody to love me. I could move on to a much healthier place than I had been in for quite some time, and it felt amazing.

Shortly after making this decision, I checked the mail without expecting to hear anything from my mother or sister. That was when I came across a letter from a friend of mine:

Dear Emma,

My heart aches for you and your family. I know that serious conflicts do not remain unchanged; they improve, or they get worse.

Your mom has caused serious damage to the people around her. Any chance of Janet being accepted and welcomed by those who love you is gone.

Neither your mom nor Janet anticipated suffering consequences over their decision, but they were wrong. Janet is one person. She cannot provide the love and care for your mom in place of all those who have been there for her over many years. They nurtured your mother in ways that Janet simply cannot replicate.

I'm hopeful that the far-reaching outcome of your mother's actions will force her to face up to the damage she has caused. I'm sure that isolation is a great motivator, giving her plenty of time to think about and regret all that she has done. Janet cannot provide her with hope. She was complicit in what she did. She cannot be everything to your mother. Your mother traded in a relationship that had lasted for a lifetime for one that was mere months old.

One more thought: If the opportunity for healing arrives, James and your children may not be willing to forgive and forget. They've seen the toll this has taken on you. They have a biased opinion. Their love for you doesn't have room for them to forgive after seeing you so hurt.

Ask your dad to pray for you. You're not abandoned. His love did not stop with his death. God bless. Don't lose hope.

Love,

Judy

I was shocked when I read that for the first time.

It felt like God's little acknowledgment of my situation, allowing me to be filled in on everything once I'd chosen to let it go. But it was also surprising to me to read about the fallout of my mother and Janet's decision. It impacted many more people beyond me and my family.

I was relieved to hear that people close to me were supportive of me, but I also didn't expect the degree of isolation my mother and Janet experienced. Given my mother's charming and manipulative behaviors, I almost wondered if there would be more people on her side. Based on Judy's letter, it didn't sound as though that was the case.

It was a bittersweet feeling. On the one hand, I felt vindicated. I knew this whole turn of events was wrong, despite my mother and Janet not seeing it that way (at least, not enough to stop them from making Janet the executor). But on the other hand, I felt disturbed. The image of my mother sitting by herself at home with no one but Janet to talk to was off-putting to me, even if they had done it to themselves.

When I thought about it a bit more, I also recognized that I could finally bask in a bit more guiltless freedom from my mother for the first time in my life. I'd often wished that I could have distance from her, but my dutiful sense of only child obligation made me feel like I always needed to be there for her. Now, there was no pressure. She had made her decision to write me out. It wasn't up to me to make the move to reconcile my relationship with her. She could do that if she felt she was ready. And I had no expectations of that happening anytime soon.

So, that was it. I was prepared never to hear another word from my mother or Janet again.

Chapter 23:

All Aboard the Gravy Train

I may not have heard from my mother or Janet directly, but I definitely heard about things my mother said through the grapevine.

They were all lies, of course, mostly directed toward my husband. She needed to have external validation that she's done the right thing, so she tried to make him look like the bad guy. She blamed him for the entire situation in an effort to get people to dislike him.

But she didn't stay there. Going beyond this specific incident, she started spreading rumors about him that ranged from annoying little habits to serious actions that someone would report if they were true. The worst one I heard was that she went around telling people that James would beat me. There could be nothing further from the truth. I swear on my father's grave that this has never happened.

Thankfully, people didn't believe her rumors; at least not from what I heard. Judy's letter served as confirmation of this, but I had trusted sources who were good and honest people. They may have wanted to agree with me anyway, but they would've also told me if she had said anything they found concerning. Plus, most people who knew me also knew her fairly well, and they had a pretty good sense of my mother's tendencies. They knew they couldn't take her at her word and mostly used me as confirmation of that.

I came across a quote from an anonymous source, which said that "Sometimes, people have to pretend you're a bad person so they don't feel guilty about the things they did to you" (in Rodenhizer, 2017, para. 1). This resonated with me so deeply. My mother has a history of stretching the truth to the point where her stories were just flat-out lies. It's what allowed her to make so many friends and what drew various men to her. She could say and do just the right things to make people believe that she wanted them around, only to ditch them or turn their lives into a living hell once they served no purpose to her.

I still don't know if she genuinely believed that she was being truthful or if she knew the real story but fabricated the lies in an effort to make her look good. She had been doing this for so long that it was hard to make that distinction. She also maintained an emotional barrier from me, so I could never really tell what she was feeling other than anger. However, when she finally revealed the truth to me about Janet being the executor over the phone, it gave me a glimpse into the possibility that she always knew what the real truth was. She just wanted to deny it and convince everyone around her that they were wrong and she was right. It's a bit eerie to think about how someone can feel so comfortable living in a lie and so uncomfortable acknowledging the truth.

Whatever she believed, she certainly had no problem making me or my husband out to be terrible people. I don't think many people who knew me believed her lies as they pertained to me over the years, but it still hurt me to think they were circulating out there. I never wanted people to think that there was even a hint of a possibility that those lies would be true. Thankfully, the people who mattered most to me never wavered in their loyalty to me. I have some of the greatest friends and family members in the world.

But part of the reason their loyalty remained consistent was that they could witness the actions of my husband and me to see how we conducted ourselves around her. They knew that I was in a complicated position being her daughter and all, but I tried to pick the polite and civil route where it was possible. They made comments over the years about how badly they felt for me that I was put in that situation. It was nice of them to acknowledge the way I had to bend over backward to please her at times.

James was the newer element, relatively speaking, but he was always good to her. He was always supportive of me going to visit her as well as her coming to stay with us. He took care of her car as well as little things around her house. He gave a speech at her birthday party. He helped out a lot when my dad was sick and stood by my mother during my father's funeral. The list is long when it comes to the various ways that James has supported my mother over the years.

There was one occasion when she was at our house for a few days in a row, sleeping in a room she had to herself. This was something she did often; case in point, we had the room painted on a previous occasion to the color she'd asked for since she stayed in there fairly regularly. But on this night, at around 8:00, she decided to call it a night. My husband poked his head into her room before she'd fallen asleep.

"Hi, Doris," he said as he tapped on her door. "I just wanted to say good night before you went off to sleep."

"Oh, I won't be sleeping for a little while," she said. "I have a hard time getting to sleep these days. Usually, I'd watch TV when I couldn't sleep at home, but I'm not exactly sure how I'll manage that tonight."

"I'm sorry to hear that," James replied. "I want you to be able to get your rest."

"Ah, well, what can ya do?" she said.

She hadn't made that comment in a rude way that demanded James do something about it, but he had other ideas. James decided that he wanted to make her arrangements more comfortable when she stayed with us, both that night and in the future.

After that conversation, my husband ran out to buy a new TV. Then, he came home and set it up that same night, even though he had to be up very early for work the next morning. He has always been so generous, sometimes to a fault. But my mother was so excited to have something in our house that reminded her of her own space. It just put everyone at ease to know that she'd be comfortable, and a TV was a small price to pay for that. And that has always been James—someone who wouldn't hesitate to step in and serve someone when they needed help.

And the TV purchase was just one of the many things he did for my mother. For context, since getting married some 30-odd years ago, my husband and I have hosted most holidays at our house. We have the most space to accommodate friends and family, and I always enjoyed having people over. It was a tradition that started through the apartment parties in my young adult years and continued on until this day.

While there were many great parts of hosting, one of my favorite parts involved being in the kitchen. My husband and I would always work hard to prepare a delicious menu and ensure it was pleasurable for everyone. Turkey, stuffing, potatoes, gravy, greens, pies… we would go all out. It was a great opportunity to work alongside James and do something that served our family. That said, it wouldn't really count for much if the guests weren't happy—okay if one guest wasn't happy.

My mother would always be in attendance, of course. Given her distaste for the meals that my paternal grandmother used to make for her (despite them being delicious), I would be a bit worried about my mother's reactions to my food. I didn't think she took issue with my cooking, but it was *my* food, after all. It wouldn't surprise me if my mother found something "wrong" with it, but James and I would do our best to give her a meal that she'd enjoy. I suppose the issues she may have had with our food weren't big enough to deter her from coming to future family gatherings.

After the fight had happened, my mother spent the following Thanksgiving with Janet. It was the first major holiday that my mom didn't spend with me and my family since I'd become an adult. Although my mother and I weren't speaking with each other at this point, I heard from some trusted sources that she'd made her feelings known about the meal she had with Janet:

"That was the best Thanksgiving meal I've ever had."

I could only smirk. It wasn't even surprising or shocking anymore. I'm glad that she finally had a good meal after 30 years.

I'm sure the food was great, but I also knew that my mother was playing up her excitement. Ever since our first meeting with Janet, my mom has been hyper-conscious of making a good impression in front of her, specifically in trying to be a loving and supportive mother. I know that might sound harsh, but after having witnessed her behavior over the years, I can safely say that she had never praised me for anything with the same amount of pride. And I mean no offense to the cooks when I say this, but this was a Thanksgiving meal that she was getting all enamored about, not even a huge milestone of some kind.

It was irritating, but at the same time, I didn't really care. My mother would always try to gain as much "gravy" as she could from a situation, which would usually come in the form of attention or status, or both. In this case, she wanted literal gravy and the love of her first daughter, so she tried to flaunt that as ostentatiously as she could.

It still wasn't enough for my mother. She had to tear me and my husband down as she attempted to lift herself up. Author Jill Blakeway (in Davenport, 2022) also had a quote that I really resonated with: "When a toxic person can no longer control you, they will try to control how others see you. The misinformation will feel unfair, but stay above it, trusting that other people will eventually see the truth, just like you did" (para. 37). Such a poignant sentiment. Thankfully, as I said, most people saw the truth because actions truly speak louder than words.

Case in point, my mother sold her home. It was a very affordable and modest space that I thought was perfect for her in her older age. Practically speaking, it didn't make sense to me to hear that she'd sold it. But the more significant part of this story comes from the fact that my mother had long said that she would never sell her home as long as she was alive.

This was probably a big reason why a lot of people who knew me didn't end up trusting my mom. Even when I had nothing to do with a given situation, she had a hard time keeping her story straight, especially as she aged. She didn't become ill or anything like that, but as she got older, I think she found it harder to remember what she said and didn't say. My friends and family members could see that. She was digging her own hole and ostracizing people around her as a result.

In place of her former home, my mother had a new house built. It was three times the size of the old one and was located very close to Janet.

I have no idea why a woman in her late 70s would want a bigger house when she'd be living in it by herself. That would just mean more cleaning and space to have to occupy with things (I suppose she could've gotten a cleaner to come in, but that's still extra work). Maybe it was meant to be a display of how much wealth she had or ensure that she could live out her final years in a luxurious environment. She always did like to show off in front of Janet, so moving into this house would fit right into that theory. Maybe she wanted to stay active and therefore walk around a larger space so that she could keep moving. Those are possible motivations, but I believe the truth lies much deeper than that.

I think she was leaning full tilt into her relationship with Janet, turning her into the daughter she felt like she never had. My mother told someone she had to move closer to Janet because she was the only one who could take care of her if she needed anything. And the larger house was also an intentional purchase. Apparently, she claimed that she needed the bigger house "now that she had a bigger family." Janet's family was much bigger than mine, so my mother wanted to accommodate them. I believe that's all true. Firstly, a bigger space would mean having more family over at the same time to center their attention on her and her lovely home. And secondly, I don't think she had any other choice. It wasn't like she could realistically invite many other people over.

Meanwhile, more and more people had been approaching me to let me know of their support for me. Although I don't know if my mother ever found out about that, she must've noticed others distancing themselves from her.

If someone had told me about her new living arrangement a few years ago, I would've been riddled with guilt. I would've felt responsible for contributing to her loneliness, even when there wasn't anything to be responsible for. I'd come to terms with the fact that I'd made the more loving gesture by being honest with her, but I would've felt weird imagining her in that state.

Yet, at this point, I felt... nothing. Not happy, not sad. It was just something I accepted, like an objective fact rather than a subjective feeling. I was a bit surprised at my lack of reactivity to hearing about the news. Still, I think I'd also spent too much time being emotionally exhausted by the situation to get invested in my mother's life again. I was sad to learn that the old house was gone, sure, but it didn't faze me at all to learn that my mother had left the house she said she'd never leave. It was par for the course. *Well*, I thought, *good to know that my mother hasn't changed.*

But despite my feelings toward her, I told my children from the very beginning to stay in touch with my mother. I assured them that what happened was between me and her. It didn't involve them, and I didn't want it to involve them. First of all, it wasn't their problem, and secondly, I didn't want my mother to think that I was using my children as pawns in some weird mind game by keeping them away from her. I'd never do that, but it wouldn't be past my mother to think that.

Sadly, it was never the same between my kids and my mother. Since she wasn't coming to my house anymore, it was harder for them to see her. My children did reach out sporadically, but they couldn't totally put things behind them. Poor kids. I feel terrible that they had to be around to witness this. They're such great people who put others ahead of themselves, which meant that they wanted the best for me. My heart swells just to think about them, and I really am sad that they don't have the same relationship with my mother. She was the only grandparent they had left, but now, it was like they didn't have any grandparents. It kind of felt like they had divorced parents—they'd spend most of their time with me and occasionally visit my mother by themselves. I was always the one making plans to bring everyone together, but that all changed.

But, as the old adage says, life goes on.

Chapter 24:

The Years That Followed

Our family found our new rhythms without Janet or my mother around.

Since Janet had only been in the picture for a few months before the blow-up, it wasn't as dramatic a transition to make with her. She hadn't been fully integrated into our lives yet; we hadn't even spent a major holiday together at that point. Not having my mother around took some getting used to, but we slowly established new patterns.

A lot of it involved returning to old patterns that had been in place before anybody knew about Janet, which took some readjusting. It was hard to go back to the way things were once we had this additional knowledge. A part of me still wondered if that would be it between me and her, but I knew I couldn't spend any more time fussing about that. I had to get back to work.

I worked at the same company for about 20 years at this point. I loved my job. I wouldn't have stayed at the company for so long if I didn't love it. I'm not someone who can just put in their 9-5 hours and clock out at the end of the day without any kind of attachment to the kind of work I did. If I was going to work somewhere, it had to be in a healthy environment with awesome coworkers, completing tasks and assignments that instilled a sense of purpose in me. That's what I had at this company.

My boss was truly the best boss ever. He was a supportive leader without being a micromanager, providing clear direction while being a warm and engaging presence. He brought our team closer together. And because I worked for a boss like that, it made me want to go the extra mile to see him and our team succeed. I put in 110% of myself every day and then some. I even worked extra hours in the evenings, on weekends, and on vacation, but I didn't mind. I wanted to reciprocate his kindness by making him look good. Plus, I thought of my job as my second home.

Isn't it true that we feel a greater sense of purpose when we're working for something beyond ourselves? I certainly felt that way about my job. Of course, I wanted to have the satisfaction of knowing that I'd done the best I could, but it was really the betterment of my colleagues that motivated me to do even better. They were the kind of people I just wanted to root for in all areas of life. My success would be their success, and vice versa. I felt the same way when I started my family and experienced the joys of life through my kids. And since my workplace was like a second home, I thought of my colleagues as professional brothers and sisters who deserved the highest levels of success.

Unfortunately, not everybody thought the same way.

A new regime took over our company that brought a different leadership style and direction from what we were used to. Basically, that's a nicer way of saying that the executives thought they were smarter and generally better than everyone else, which was far from accurate. Once they came on board, our happy little team didn't stand much of a chance against people who thought they knew better and weren't willing to hear us out.

For starters, they laid off my boss through no fault of his own. They just felt that he was disposable and that they wanted to go in a "different direction." Don't they all?

Hearing about my now-former boss packing up his things and walking out the door was a gut punch of a day. At that moment, no one on our team felt safe. If the new leadership team was willing to nix someone like him so quickly and readily, we had no idea what that meant for the rest of us. It was certainly a bit of a bad omen.

My first interaction with the new leadership team wasn't something that brought on much more hope, either. One of the members of the leadership team had planned to have a little meeting with me, which revealed exactly where her priorities stood.

"You wanted to see me?" I asked, standing in the doorway to her office.

The leader sat at her desk, which faced the door, staring at her computer screen. She knew I was waiting for her, but she completely ignored me. Instead, she just kept looking at her computer as I stood there, waiting for her to respond.

Well, I knew I had to meet with her eventually. After she'd refused to acknowledge my presence, I walked into her office as she kept staring at her computer. Then, she got up and walked out. She didn't look at me or even say a word to me. She just left.

I didn't know what to do. Was she coming back? Was I supposed to follow her? I ended up just standing there out of confusion and frustration. It was outrageously rude.

After a few minutes, she did come back and got right down to business, still without any pleasantries at all.

"So… When are you planning on retiring?"

I just stood there stunned. This was my first interaction with her, and she was already asking me when I was going to retire. Was that even legal?

"Umm, well, I didn't have an exact date in mind at this point," I responded. "I'd like to continue working here for as long as it's feasible to do so." It wasn't like I was some senior citizen working way past my retirement time. I wasn't even at retirement age.

She leaned forward in her chair. "Well, you see, you make a lot of money with the company. I'm sure you do a fine job at whatever it is you do, but, well, you make a lot more than anyone else who does the same job in my department. So…"

I waited to see if she was going to finish that sentence. Rather than being left on a cliffhanger, I decided to get to the bottom of the matter.

"Well, what's the longest amount of time someone has worked in your department here?" I asked.

She thought for a second. "About 10 years, maybe?"

"I've been here for 20. Wouldn't it make sense that I make more money than them?"

"No, that's not how it works."

"Why not?"

"You shouldn't be expecting any raises in the near future."

I was baffled at the level of unprofessionalism, but I didn't want to get into a fight. I had to find a civil-enough way to end it while holding my ground.

"Well, I want to be honest with you in saying that I have no plans on leaving, and I hope we can find some kind of working relationship with one another." I practically spoke out of my teeth in an effort to control my temper. I couldn't lose my cool while she was forming her first impression of me; otherwise, I'd have the same fate as my old boss.

But she had another bomb to drop.

"Well, then, is there a reason why you don't come into the office anymore?" she asked, thinking I'd be thrown off by the question. I wasn't.

"Yes, there is. I've been working from home for the last six years, give or take. Honestly, I've found that I can put in way more hours at home than I can coming to the office from 9-5. It saves me a commute, and my boss didn't mind—"

"I don't think you can efficiently do your job at home. Starting immediately, you'll need to report back to the office every day."

"But I just told you that I can work from home. I get *more* work done from home."

"I'm sure you'd like that, wouldn't you?" she smirked, looking back at her computer. "You can go now."

I never even had to sit down at her desk. That's how quick the "meeting" was.

I walked away from that conversation feeling terribly unsettled. This felt like the start of a very dark chapter in our company's existence, and I was not looking forward to how everything would unfold.

At first, I received my vindication. COVID hit a few months later, causing everyone to have to work from home. Oh, the beautiful irony of it all. Funnily enough, I was still able to get all my work done.

But the next year was the year from hell.

This merciless leadership team kept reporting people who had been loyal employees for years, which subsequently meant a lot of backstabbing and game-playing. It was truly a toxic work environment.

These were wicked, wicked people who seemed to have no sense of conscience in betraying people left and right. Everything had to be done their way, even though their way was poorly designed and impractical. But it didn't matter because they thought very highly of themselves and wouldn't entertain any other suggestions. They'd try to disguise everything under a smile or an upbeat attitude, but we all knew there was a lot more happening behind the scenes. They were sure not to tell the veterans about those discussions until the decisions had been made, and it was too late to change anything about it.

Other than my team members whom I'd known for years, I had no idea who I could trust. There is nothing worse than people who act nice to your face but are planning your demise in the meantime. I honestly don't know how those kinds of people can sleep at night, knowing all of the people and families they had to burn in an effort to hold onto any kind of power. Yet, they found a way to keep doing it.

Imagine coming to work one day with a whole new set of bosses telling you everything you've done for the last 20 years is wrong. I got nervous and defensive at first, but after I realized what was happening, I couldn't take the feedback I received seriously. The new leadership team had a personal vendetta against a lot of the older staff, particularly those with higher salaries. Maybe they were trying to drive us out by putting us through hell. If that was the case, they certainly tried their hardest.

A few of the newer employees who had some access to the leadership team's decisions warned me about their next move.

"You'll be the next to go," they said to me.

By that point, the comment nearly made me laugh. The novelty of their cruel ways had worn off by that point, and I was preparing for that inevitable call to their office. I didn't hide the fact that I didn't like them. They had become caricatures of these cartoonish villains who only cared about power and success and not the people who helped them get that recognition. I almost couldn't take them seriously anymore. I certainly didn't feel the need to put in the same amount of work for the new regime as I did for my old boss because of their terrible attitudes.

Sure enough, one year after my boss was let go, they let me go, too. I was three years away from my retirement.

How right those employees were.

I was ready for it, though. I had cleaned out my desk and cleared everything from my computer long before I got the call. I would just sit at my desk waiting for it by the end.

I knew from my first interaction with them that they did not want either me or my ex-boss to be in their department. The two of us did not fit in with that group of people nor their vision for the company. But I refused to quit, no matter how much I hated working for them. After working at that company for as long as I had, I wanted a solid package upon my departure. I got one. It felt like as much justice as I could get after the miserable year I'd spent working for those lying manipulators.

That being said, it was just the one year that made my life absolutely miserable (and there was a lot more going on with my mother and Janet during that time which heightened my misery). Before the changeover had happened, it was an excellent company to work for. There was a culture of mutual trust and camaraderie. We knew that we were all in this together in wanting to make a quality product that made us all proud. We knew that the old leadership team was going to look after us, and they knew that we would look out for them in return. There was a sense of belonging, a sense of structure, and a sense of family.

Part of that familial feeling that we shared came from the sense of honesty that we all shared with one another. We all had a say when we felt that something wasn't right. We could certainly bring up our criticisms or concerns without fear of getting fired. That's part of what it takes to be in a family: a sense of respect.

By respecting one another's opinions, we didn't feel threatened by others' viewpoints when they put their thoughts on the table. Leadership certainly didn't feel like their intelligence or anything was under attack; if anything, they celebrated the fact that we felt comfortable enough to speak up on an issue. They'd much rather have criticisms raised during a private meeting and make the necessary changes right away. The alternative would involve publicly embarrassing the leadership staff because no one felt they could challenge their authority. No one wanted that. For years, the company had been admired for its excellence, but once the changeover happened, it wasn't thought of as highly anymore.

As the changeover was happening, the focus of the company was no longer on the product; it was on the numbers. More specifically, it was about increasing sales with fewer workers. They purchased cheaper materials and sliced the staff team until it was a fraction of what it used to be. Everyone was expected to do even more work. The environment completely changed into a space that didn't have an ounce of respect for the company's process or employees. One of the executives, in their infinite wisdom, even decided to move one of the plants to another state. Many hard-working people who had been there for years were now out of a job because this particular individual had a whim of thought entirely motivated by money. I don't know how they expected people to settle for this, but somehow, people did.

I felt sorry for those who settled, whether or not they believed they had a way out. Perhaps that was part of the reason why I had no problem speaking my mind at that point. I knew that I had been a loyal employee for two decades and that the people who knew me at the company knew the integrity of my character and work ethic. I had spent enough years in the workforce to know good leadership from poor leadership, along with the motivations for poor leadership. They didn't threaten me, and they knew that.

However, I didn't want to spend my retirement focusing on revenge. It dawned on me that the pursuit of revenge is almost like an addiction. When you initially get your revenge, it feels so satisfying in the moment to see someone get their comeuppance. They've done you wrong, and they're finally paying for it. But once that initial thrill wears off, it doesn't seem like enough. You feel like they deserve worse. You can't help but remember the ways in which they've hurt you. You feel like they need even greater punishment for that. And yet, no matter how much punishment they receive, it won't ever make up for the pain you felt. Pretty soon, you're just focusing your life on waiting around to see someone fail, which turns you into a self-righteous and miserable person. I didn't want to become that.

I do believe that everyone will have to address their wrongdoings at some point, but in my retirement, I wanted to concentrate on the good I could still contribute to the world. I'd already learned the hard lesson of letting go of the things that would turn me into an anxious wreck. I didn't want to sacrifice this hard-earned retirement in order to be a vengeful, hate-filled person. That wouldn't be fair to my husband or children. So, instead of focusing on the pain of my past, I wanted to focus on the joy of my present and future. And that's exactly what I did.

That was a glorious period of my life. I not only reveled in the joy of being free from the clutches of horrible executives, but I could instead dedicate that time to people who refreshed me and filled me with love. My husband and I spent more quality time together, I could spend more time with my children, and I had more time to reconnect with friends like Amy and Carin. I also had more time to do things that I never had the time to do before. For the first time in a long while, I felt truly relaxed. My mind, body, and soul could all take a deep sigh of relief. Everything was okay.

Then, one day, I was spending some time with myself when I heard my phone ring. I took a look at the caller ID and froze.

It was my mother.

Chapter 25:

Call Waiting, Part 2

My eyes had never been wider.

I just stared at the name "Mom" on my phone screen.

Ring.

My face went beet red. My heart rate soared.

What should I do? I haven't spoken to her in three years. Should I pick it up? What would I say?

Ring.

I didn't know what to do. So many thoughts scattered through my mind, and I couldn't make sense of any of them.

Is she okay? I don't want to talk to her. But what if this is my last chance? No, she burned that bridge a long time ago. But what if she's had a change of heart?

Ring.

Finally, one thought surfaced through the wave of confusion:

If you don't pick it up now, you'll spend the rest of your life wondering what she would've said.

Ring.

I knew that was the right thought, which is what scared me so much. But I didn't have time to think about that. I took a deep breath and tapped the green button.

"Hello?"

"Hi."

"Hi, Mom."

A little pause. I couldn't believe that I was actually hearing her voice again. It all made my stomach twist into knots.

"Uh, how are you?" I managed to spit out.

"Good, good," she said. "It's been too long since we've done this."

"Yeah, it's been three years…"

"I do hope we can get past this. I don't want some argument to get in the middle of our relationship."

"Well, that's—yeah, it would be nice to move on from that." I stopped myself from letting my knee-jerk reaction come through, which would've involved telling her that this wasn't just "some argument." But I was still shocked that she had even called me in the first place and wanted to give the conversation a chance to go somewhere. So, I held my tongue as I listened to my mother exhale on the other end of the phone.

"Emma, I don't want to live without you in my life."

To this day, I think that's the nicest thing she ever said to me. It seemed like the closest she'd come to telling me that she loved me. Her comment almost hit my ears funny because I wasn't accustomed to hearing her say something so nice about my role in her life. She wanted *me* around? Crazy.

But on top of the message itself, I found the timing of the message to be quite striking. She said this to me within the first minute or two of our conversation. There hadn't been some big emotional gesture beforehand that prompted her to say that in the heat of the moment. Instead, she said it right away in a very calm manner, perhaps with a hint of longing in her voice. By my mother's standards, that's quite withdrawn. It made me wonder if something had happened to her or if she was unwell because I wasn't expecting this to happen.

"Wow, Mom, that was… really nice of you to say," I began. "I'll admit, when you called me today, I wasn't really sure what to expect, but… it's nice to hear from you."

"It's nice to hear your voice," she responded.

Another brief pause. I had so many thoughts that had been lying dormant for three years that were just starting to awaken. I figured this could be a good chance to entertain some of the questions I'd had for years.

"Mom, can I ask you something?"

"Sure."

"I mean… There's just been so much on my mind since our last conversation, and now that you're here… I'm wondering if I can just talk to you about them in total honesty. Is that okay?"

She paused for a second or two. "I would be okay with that."

"You're not gonna like everything I have to say, just so you know. I have a lot to say to you, and I don't know how much of it is gonna be positive."

"Anything you'd like."

"You're sure?"

"Go ahead."

I'd tried to give her as many warnings as I could. I still wasn't really sure what was going to come out of my mouth, but if this conversation was going to go in the same direction as the last one, I wanted to make sure I had my bases covered. She knew what was on my mind, and she'd given her permission to proceed. *Okay*, I thought, *there's no way she can blame me for anything if things go south now…*

"Do you think you overreacted about the whole shoe thing?"

There. I said it. Now, I wait to see what she—

"Yes."

My jaw nearly hit the floor. She said *yes*? *My* mother said *yes*?

"Umm, wow, okay, I didn't know you felt that way about it," I fumbled over my words.

"Well, it was really just a stupid incident that got blown out of proportion," she said.

"I agree. It really wasn't that big of a deal."

"No, it wasn't. Certainly, not one big enough to get a mother and a daughter to stop talking to one another."

"Okay, well, about that. After we stopped talking, I'd heard that there were rumors being spread about James hitting me. Do you know anything about that?"

Her lips smacked. "No, I've never heard about that before."

Hmm. "You don't remember saying anything about that to anyone?"

"What? No, not at all."

Okay, so my mother was still my mother. I knew she was lying to me by not fessing up to spreading those rumors, which annoyed me. I hated the thought of her slandering James' name like that and not owning up to it, but I still wanted to hold back. There was a lot more to be explored in this conversation, and I didn't want to blow it now.

"How is work going?" she asked me. She wasn't one to ask many questions about my life, so I knew she must've really wanted to extend an olive branch—well, maybe not a full branch, but at least an olive twig.

"Well, that's a story in itself… I got laid off."

"Oh, no, what happened?"

"New leadership came in and took the company in a totally different direction. They fired my boss pretty much right away, and it was only a matter of time before they'd let me go, too."

"Oh, Emma."

"Yeah. Three years before I was due for my retirement, too."

"I'm so sorry to hear that."

"Yeah, well, it wasn't all bad. They were terrible leaders. So many mind games and backstabbing… It was just awful."

I realized as I made those remarks that my mother had done the exact same thing to me over the years, which made me hesitate for a second. But then I thought, *No, she needs to know that this kind of behavior isn't acceptable. Maybe she could learn from this.*

"Oh, no," she said. "It sounds like they let you go at a pretty good time, then."

"Yeah, I mean, it would've been nice to end my career on a high note, but that sure wasn't going to happen in that environment. I'm just glad that the bulk of my time there was enjoyable and positive."

"Yes, that's true."

"And James actually retired not too long ago, too. So, the two of us have been spending more time together, which has been really nice."

"Oh, that's wonderful. Good for him. He's been working hard for so many years now. He deserves to be retired."

Wow. A surprisingly kind reaction. I wasn't sure how it would go over for me to bring up James in our conversation, but so far, it seemed okay. Phew.

"Thanks, yeah, it's been great," I said.

"It's nice that you two can enjoy your retirements at the same time."

"Yeah, for sure." Although things were going well with James as the subject of conversation, I didn't want to entertain too much more of it, just in case.

"How are the kids?" my mom asked.

"They're good. They're growing up so fast. I mean, I know they're adults now, but it still hits me sometimes, like, 'Oh my gosh, you're so big!' I know they probably wouldn't appreciate me saying that to them, but I can't help myself."

My mother laughed at that. At least, I think it was a laugh. So many things caught me off guard up until this point that I wasn't sure what to make of them. I was still waiting for the other shoe to drop.

"Yeah, they must be making their way through the world now."

"They really are. It's scary! But I'm so happy for them."

"You have a lot to be proud of in them."

"Thanks, I do feel a lot of pride. They're great kids."

"That's good, that's really good. You should come see my new house now that you have more time on your hands."

I wasn't quite sure how to respond to that. I tried to address that without giving a direct answer.

"Yeah, I heard that you'd moved. So, you like it, then?"

"Oh, yeah, it's great. There's so much more space to... have people over."

Ha. *People.* Well played.

"Well, it must be a nice place if it managed to take you away from the old house. I remember when you and Dad first moved in there. It's still a bit crazy to me to think about how you're not living there anymore."

"I know, but that chapter came to a close. It was time for something new."

"Yeah, but sometimes the old can still serve a purpose. So many memories were made in the old."

"Sure, but I'm really enjoying the new. I've always liked the new. Although… I guess revisiting the old from time to time isn't so bad."

I had a feeling we weren't talking about the houses anymore.

"But if you wanted to move so badly, why didn't you just rent an apartment?" I asked her. "It would've been way easier, especially at your age."

"Hmm, yeah, that might have been a good idea," she responded. "You always give me good ideas."

Huh. That was my first time hearing that one. Alright then.

"Well, at least you got that all sorted out," I said.

"Yeah, it has been a good change. Especially since COVID hit."

"Oh, yeah, I could imagine."

We talked about COVID-19 for a bit. I realized this would've been a good opening for me to see if she'd gotten sick or had other major news to break to me. She didn't break anything.

It was only at this moment that I started to accept the fact that my mother just wanted to talk to me. I'd just become so defensive against her ulterior motives over the years that I'd prepared myself for the worst. Between my history with my mother and simply getting older myself, I'd become more skeptical and cynical in my interactions with her out of protection. I didn't want to bare my heart to her if I didn't think she was sincere. I'd been burned too many times by trying to do that.

Once I accepted the fact that I was just having a catch-up with my mom, it was actually quite a nice conversation. It felt like what mother-daughter relationships were supposed to feel like. Of course, I was still a little bit guarded, but I felt more relaxed with her than I'd felt... maybe ever?

Wow, it has actually been really nice to chat with my mom again, I thought to myself.

"I feel like we should be doing more of this," my mother said to me. "I miss this. I miss you."

That caused a new thought to pop up: Could I potentially mend my relationship with my mother? Since she'd already permitted me to be totally honest with her, I thought this could be my chance.

"Well, Mom, it would be really nice to keep doing this regularly with you," I began, "but I'll have to be honest with you; I don't think I could move forward with our relationship unless some things change."

"What do you mean?" my mother asked.

"Well, namely, that you change your will back to the way it was before. So that I'd be the executor instead of Janet."

I think that caught her off guard. She hesitated for a moment.

"Well, how can I do that now?"

"What do you mean? You can go back to the lawyer's office again, can't you?"

"Sure, I mean, legally, there wouldn't be an issue. But it's just that Janet already knows that she is the executor now. It wouldn't be right to just change that on her."

Did she know who she was talking to?

"Well, you can do to her what you did to me. You could just change the executorship and not tell her about it."

My mom didn't say anything to that.

"She'd find out after you pass away," I said.

To be clear, I wasn't saying this in an attempt to be vengeful or vindictive. I truly believe what I said in the last chapter about not wanting to seek revenge on people who'd hurt me, and that includes my mother. Being the executor of my mother's will was never about the money for me. I didn't want anything. It was about the principle of the matter, along with my father's legacy.

I simply could not accept Janet being in charge of my father's estate. He'd worked so hard for his whole life to earn everything he ever got, only to die of a horrible death and not be able to enjoy most of it. The money he'd made during the time would now be managed by a woman who he didn't even know existed: A woman who was conceived out of an affair behind his back. He did not deserve that.

Even still, when I made the suggestion to my mother, she didn't have much to say to that. She paused for a bit longer than usual.

"I'll think about it," she said. "I'll get back to you."

That was about as positive of a response as I could've hoped for. I was elated but tried to temper that emotion over the phone.

"That sounds great, thank you. I really appreciate this, Mom. It would just mean a lot to me to have the final say on what happened with Dad's estate."

"Yeah."

Silence.

"Well, Emma, it's been great," my mother said. "I'm very thankful that you picked up the phone today."

"I'm thankful that you called, Mom. It has been really nice to talk to you, and I look forward to hearing from you about the will."

"Yes, I'll let you know. Take care, Emma."

"You too, Mom. Bye."

"Bye."

Call ended.

I breathed a sigh of relief. That went shockingly well. For the first time in years, I had a genuinely nice conversation with my mother. There were a few moments when things were getting a little tense, but all in all, I couldn't have asked for anything more. It was a breath of fresh air.

And, to top it all off, she said she was willing to think over everything with her will. I was brimming with optimism after hearing that response. I felt so good about our future and couldn't wait to hear back.

So, I waited a day. No call. *Okay*, I thought, *maybe she needs more time to think about it. Fair enough.*

Another day passed. Nothing.

Another day. Nothing.

A week.

Two weeks.

A month.

Many more months.

All nothing.

It didn't take long for me to realize there was a good chance she had no plans to call me any time soon. Instead, I was left to sit with the thought that I'd potentially had my last conversation with my mother.

Epilogue:

Forgiveness

I never did hear from my mom again.

I don't know if she knew this would be her final conversation with me going into that phone call, but that's certainly what came out of it. I often wondered if that was why she'd been much softer with me in that chat than she'd been in the past. If she knew she wouldn't talk to me again, maybe she wanted to make sure that it was a pleasant one.

The realization met me with a wave of disappointment. After that conversation, I'd felt so hopeful that things would be taking a turn for the better, only to be left in a similar place of despair. Of course, I went over my own words in my head, wondering if I would've said anything different if I'd known it would be the last time I spoke with her. Truth be told, I don't know that I would've changed much. I was honest with her about how I felt about the situation, and she maintained a sense of politeness and civility with me. If I had to settle for a bittersweet resolution, this was a relatively good way for it to go out.

Because I didn't hear from my mother, that also led me to believe she didn't change anything about her will. This meant that Janet would still be in charge of my dad's estate, including his ashes. It still stings something fierce, but if I can try to hold onto any bit of hope in all of this, it'll be that Janet will come to her senses and do the right thing. She'd never treated me poorly to my face, and I also knew she wasn't used to my mom's manipulative ways, either. She was likely so swept up in the idea of reuniting with her biological mom again that she wanted to go along with whatever would please her. I can understand that, although I still think her actions against me were atrocious.

If Janet has any humanity, she'll return the ashes to me. I haven't spoken to her since my big fight with my mother, so I don't know everything that has been said about me to her over the years. I hope she has the kind of conscience that would allow me this one token of my father's estate. One can certainly hope.

Before I learned anything about Janet, I think I had a very conventional understanding of what it meant to have—and be—a family. I often associate it with the biological tie that brings most people together, which I think is the classical definition that many correlate with family. As I've had more time to reflect on this subject, I've also reconsidered the emotional tie that comes into play with families. In the case of adopted or blended families, this is especially crucial in bringing people together.

My situation had felt like a tug of war between both sides, particularly when it came to being a sister. People like Amy and Carin made me yearn for a sister when I was young because of all the fun times we shared together in spite of our biological separation. I might've referred to them as my "sisters" in the sense of being a close female friend, but I still considered myself to be an only child for 54 years. Yet, when I met Janet later on, I was initially elated by the thought of having a biological sibling. As time went on, though, I discovered that I could not trust her nearly as much as I could trust my female friends, which complicated the subject even further for me.

So, what does it mean to be a family?

As I write this, I believe it has more to do with the sense of loyalty that we have to certain people in our lives. To be clear, I don't want to suggest that relationships should just be a transactional, tit-for-tat kind of matter. As I said in a previous chapter, there will be times when things get a little one-sided if someone is going through a busy season of life or someone is incapable of doing a certain task. But people can still show loyalty to one another in different ways. For instance, when my kids were young, I knew I'd have to do the bulk of the cooking and cleaning for them, even though I knew they couldn't have done that for me. However, they still showed their loyalty to me by choosing to follow house rules or make me crafts at school. The sentiment is still there, even if the actions are dependent on what they're capable of doing at that time.

People can be brought together in an infinite number of ways, from sharing the same parents to sharing the same beliefs about the world. We can also form connections with any number of people that can grow and change over time. But to me, a family implies that people have intentionally vowed to come together for a shared purpose. They can still disagree and fight from time to time—all families do—but it's all being done for the greater good of those involved. In fact, because that union is so strong and the shared values are so firmly ingrained in family members, we can more easily forgive one another for whatever shortcomings come into focus.

Oprah Winfrey (in Goodreads, 2011) has defined forgiveness as "giving up the hope that the past could have been any different... accepting the past for what it was, and using this moment and this time to help yourself move forward" (para. 1). I love this definition because it acknowledges that certain events have happened without neglecting how they have affected us. I was absolutely wrecked by the actions of my mother and sister, and it's important for me to recognize that. It would also be futile to pretend that I could've done something different about it, especially given my mother's history of questionable behavior. In order for me to move forward from all of that, I have to be honest with myself about what happened in order to properly reflect on it, heal from it, and move on from it.

Similarly, life coach Cassandra Bodhi (2019) said in a video that "forgiveness is not for the other person. Forgiveness does not excuse the behavior; forgiveness does not condone the behavior" (1:33). Later in the same video when she talked about the actual process of forgiving, she said something really interesting to me: "When we forgive somebody, we're giving ourselves that gift of peace" (2:00). That hit a nerve with me because I'd spent so many years trying to please my mother to my own detriment. I'd felt like such a failure if I didn't do everything to please her, yet it felt like I could never reach that standard. Yet, when I reframed my understanding of forgiveness to focus on my own actions instead of simultaneously trying to anticipate my mother's response, I felt so much more freedom in making that decision.

Now, do I believe that forgiveness can heal relationships on both sides? Absolutely, but only if both sides are truly open to it. A relationship cannot exist (at least, a healthy one can't) unless both parties are willing to work on the broken parts of it together. That wasn't the case for me. I can only control my own actions, and by forgiving my mother, I'm releasing the burden from my end of things.

To address the question of "Where do I truly belong?" from the prologue, I'm still trying to figure that out. If someone had told me my life would've ended up like this, I wouldn't have believed them. At this point in my life, though, I believe that time is best spent with my husband, children, aunts, cousins, and friends. After the tumultuous past few years, I'm finding so much enjoyment in spending this relaxing time with people I love and can serve with my whole heart. Who knows, maybe there are new relationships on the horizon that will continue to expand my knowledge on these topics. It's certainly not out of the realm of possibility for me.

I'm also loving the retirement life that allows me to try new things along the way as well, which includes writing this book. I've wanted to do it for four years, but I never had the time to sit down and write due to working so many hours. But now, I've finally had my chance, and what a ride it has been. From the bottom of my heart, I want to thank anyone who has taken the time to read this story. It means so much to me to write down these thoughts and share them with you. Thank you.

As one last writing exercise, Cassandra Bodhi recommended that her audience members write a letter to the person that has hurt them as a way to fully admit their experience and feelings. She also stressed that they did not need to physically give the letter to the person being addressed, instead suggesting that it was meant to be a healing exercise for the writer. One could argue that this whole book has been a great long letter to my mother, but I want to spend a few moments now capturing my final thoughts in the form of a formal letter. I do not plan on giving this letter to my mother.

> Mom,
>
> We've had some bad times, but we've had some good times, too. I miss the good times. I was a good daughter to you for so many years, and I did not deserve this kind of treatment.
>
> You hurt me beyond words. I will never understand why you did what you did and why Janet went along with it. How could you abandon your daughter of 54 years and her family for someone you just met? How could you abandon *your* family who'd stuck by you through ups and downs?
>
> I could not and would not ever do that to my children, no matter the circumstances. They are too important to me, and I couldn't live without them in my life. I guess you don't feel the same way.

Why couldn't we just be one big happy family? Especially when everyone had already accepted the situation? Maybe this is the life you always wanted—a life with Janet instead of with me. Well, now you have it. I hope you are finally happy.

After all these years, I think I realize now why you never really cared for me and blamed me for things that weren't my fault. You held it against me that I was in your life, and you had to give Janet up. Could I have helped with that? It's too late to answer that now, but you never even gave me a chance to try.

Yes, I know you did these awful things to me and hurt me terribly. However, I am taking my life back today and forgiving you.

Your daughter,

Emma

"Look, I am coming soon! My reward is with me, and I will give to each person according to what they have done" (*New International Version Bible,* 2011/1978, Revelation 22:12).

Abigail can be reached via email at *Aherows44@gmail.com*

References

Bodhi, C. (2019, April 12). The art if forgiveness is an act of self love video blog is now up I hope this serves you in an amazing way . Facebook. https://www.facebook.com/watch/?v=678146862640345

Cleveland Clinic. (2020, June 19). Narcissistic personality disorder. https://my.clevelandclinic.org/health/diseases/9742-narcissistic-personality-disorder

Davenport, B. (2022, December 2). 27 toxic mother quotes that show how mom can mess you up. Live Bold and Bloom. https://liveboldandbloom.com/12/emotional-abuse/toxic-mother-quotes

Goodreads. (2020). A quote by Albert Einstein. https://www.goodreads.com/quotes/620163-the-more-i-learn-the-more-i-realize-how-much

Goodreads. (2011). A quote by Oprah Winfrey. https://www.goodreads.com/quotes/376558-forgiveness-is-giving-up-the-hope-that-the-past-could

New International Version Bible. (2011). Bible Gateway. https://www.biblegateway.com/versions/New-International-Version-NIV-Bible/#booklist (Original work published 1978)

Rodenhizer, S. (2017, March 10). "Sometimes people pretend you're a bad person so they don't feel guilty about the things they did to you." (unknown). Quotation Celebration. https://quotationcelebration.wordpress.com/2017/03/10/sometimes-people-pretend-youre-a-bad-person-so-they-dont-feel-guilty-about-the-things-they-did-to-you-unknown/

Made in United States
North Haven, CT
25 October 2023

43211262R00146